I0536762

DEAD TO DEADLY

DEAD TO DEADLY

BY

AVINDER SINGH

© 2025 Harsimran Kaur Kapoor

All rights reserved. No part of this book may be reproduced in any form or by any electronic or mechanical means, including information storage and retrieval systems, without permission in writing from the publisher, except by a reviewer, who may quote brief passages in a review.

ISBN: 978-1-0689298-3-0

First Edition

Author: Avinder Singh

Publisher: Harsimran Kaur Kapoor

Dedicated to

my father-in-law, Sardar Devinder Singh,

a renowned author himself.

I'd like to acknowledge the efforts of my wife and daughters, whose unwavering support and encouragement have propelled me forward.

This labour of love is not mine alone but theirs as well, as they read and re-read this book and suggested ways to make it better.

Preface

The story is set in the Indian province of Kashmir and Delhi in the year 2000, a year that saw the change of a century and a millennium. It is about a nondescript and ordinary employee of a small company who finds himself suddenly placed in an adverse and dangerous situation by his employer.

The story is about his struggle and ingenuity in extricating himself from this precarious and adverse situation. It is about the power he finds within himself to survive and prosper. He goes on to exploit this courage and power to achieve a meteoric rise in his career.

The story is set in an era when morality was ambiguous in India. Nothing was black or white, only shades of grey. Tax evasion was rampant, the law was lax, and most bureaucrats were corrupt. Mobile phones were not common. India's auto industry was striving for modernity.

The situation in the Kashmir Valley was politically tumultuous, with militancy being 'enjoyed' by the youth who loved the glamour that came with it. Pakistan had violated the Line of Control (interim border) to dominate and disrupt India's line of communication to Leh (Ladakh) in the summer of 1999. Pakistani terrorists had hijacked an Indian Plane to Kandahar in December that year. Pakistan Inter State Intelligence (ISI) was funding and fuelling the militancy as part of their undeclared war on India. India insisted that it was terrorism. The militants targeted innocent civilians more than the security forces. There were mass killings. Over thirty Sikhs had been massacred in March 2000. Another over ninety pilgrims were shot in August later that year in multiple incidents.

India had created special battalions called the *Rashtriya Rifles*, RR for short, which had volunteers from the regular Army to assist the local police and the administration in keeping some kind of law and order. These battalions were perpetually on seek and eliminate operations. There was a race amongst them to notch up the maximum 'kills.' The promotion of the commanding officer was invariably dependent on the number of successful operations conducted, which translated to the number of militants neutralized (killed). Intelligence was the key to such operations, and both military and civil intelligence were supposed to cooperate, but they rarely did. When they did cooperate, they achieved tangible results. Of course, there were chance encounters as well, where the militants usually had the upper hand. They either surprised the forces from village houses or from forest heights. After suffering initial losses, these locations would then be cordoned off, and more forces would be brought in to 'neutralize' the terrorists.

The central character of this story not only faced these terrorists but also exploited chance encounters with them. He went on to avenge his betrayal by destroying the nexus that worked against him, turning himself into a villain of sorts. This is a tale of survival, revenge, greed, lust, and success. It depicts the difficult conditions and circumstances under which the central character, Ajay, survives and prospers by means not entirely ethical.

DEAD TO DEADLY

Taken

May 2000

Blindfolded, I was being hauled up a slope and some rough, muddy steps. Stumbling with my hands tied, I felt helpless and scared to death. My sprained left ankle throbbed. I let it drag, less out of pain but more to slow my captors down. After what felt like ages but could not have been more than fifteen or twenty minutes, we stopped, and it appeared to my blind senses that two of my three captors had sat down. While I winced in pain and tried to catch my breath, I heard a chain being dragged and felt hands on my right ankle, a chain being wrapped around it and locked with a padlock, perhaps. While all this was happening, I recalled the conversation my captors had in Kashmiri, where one of them suggested that I wasn't important enough and that no one would respond. Meanwhile, the other insisted that the government would eventually come around. The first one vehemently expressed the fear that the Army would come looking for me and get them instead.

One of them then yelled, "Oey Raina, relax and sit down." So, they knew who I was.

What a hellish end to such a lovely day! Scenes from the past two days flashed in my mind. My boss, Mr. Khan, had called me to his office chamber.

"Ajay, you are going to Kashmir," he'd said. He had informed me that I had been chosen to select a plot of land for our upcoming project of a juice packaging facility near Sopore (Jammu & Kashmir). "Your knowledge of Kashmiri and local influence will help."

"Sir, my family left Kashmir in the 1970s. We hardly speak Kashmiri anymore," I had pointed out.

"That's okay. You're still the best person for the job. It will be like a paid holiday," he'd mused.

"When do I leave?" I'd asked.

"Plan a ten-day trip. You fly out tomorrow," he had said.

By now, I was quite excited but did not express it. The corporate world had its compulsions, but I was happy that I was about to have ten easy days. I knew my plan of action: I would select a few sites, negotiate lease amounts, complete a report with pros and cons, and be done with it.

I phoned my wife Priya to inform her about my solo trip. She protested about not being able to join me in Kashmir. To make it up to her, we went out to a small local restaurant that evening with our two children, Rohan, 14, and Rhea, 9, for a meal. It was a special night for us as a couple since I would be leaving her for a few days. The next morning, I was at Delhi Airport, preparing to fly to Srinagar. Upon arrival, I collected my one-piece luggage and exited the arrival area. Outside, I was met by a middle-aged local man holding a placard that simply read 'Mr. Ajay Raina.'

When I approached him, he asked, "Raina *sahib*?"

I nodded in response, and he took my suitcase. I held on to my briefcase and the jacket draped over my arm.

"The taxi is in the car park," he said.

I followed him to the taxi. I had booked a budget hotel in Sopore, and I told the driver the name. He said he knew the hotel where I was staying and had been hired by the hotel to pick me up. I was surprised but pleased with the office's logistics team, who had informed the hotel of my booking and thoughtfully asked my hotel to organize a taxi for me.

The ride to the hotel took around two hours, and it took us through the stunningly beautiful countryside and outskirts of Srinagar. Unfortunately, the hotel was somewhat disappointing. My carpeted room on the first floor had a musky odour, and just one window that overlooked the neglected backyard.

Although unhappy with the choice of my hotel, it would have to do. Just when I was about to open my suitcase, I heard agitated and urgent voices in Kashmiri and some commotion in the reception area. I dismissed it as some management issue and went about my business.

Before I could unlock my suitcase, I heard a rude, loud knock on my door. The moment I opened it, two masked men, one with an AK-47 type of weapon, barged in. While one of them pointed a pistol at my left temple, the other twisted my right arm backwards. They started to push and force me down the stairs, past the reception. I looked at the receptionist, horrified. He seemed aghast, too. I was taken to a van and bundled inside.

There were two more men in the van who grabbed me. One of them put a cloth on my eyes and tied the blindfold tightly. My hands, too, were tied behind me, but the knot wasn't very tight. It was a knot tied in a hurry. Just then, the engine started, and the vehicle surged. Judging by its sway on a turn, it had moved out of the hotel gate at some speed.

I knew I was taken.

Uncertain Destination

Moments later, I mustered some courage and asked in a squeaky voice and broken Kashmiri why they were doing this to me.

"What have I done?" I pleaded.

One of my abductors asked me to shut up, suffixing his sentence with Kaffir. I was in big trouble. I feared that as soon as we hit the countryside, I might be shot. I could now feel my heart pounding in my chest, my lips were dry, and panic gripped me. I tried pleading with them and begged them to let me go.

"I have two children," I said, almost sobbing.

I was utterly shocked and ashamed of my squeaky, pleading voice. I had never felt this scared in my life. I began to sob uncontrollably. I heard two of my captors laugh. I tried to feign laughter, too, while sobbing. I asked them what they wanted from me.

One of the captors replied, "A lot."

The journey to nowhere seemed never-ending. I asked for water and was told to wait. It began to dawn on me that it was all a setup. But the question was 'why?'. Why would someone want to kill me after getting me all the way from Delhi? There were enough targets within the state. Maybe it was a ransom that they wanted, or perhaps I was a hostage for an exchange. These thoughts gave me some hope. But fear and panic gripped me. I felt helpless.

After what seemed an eternity, it appeared that we were now driving off the road. The vehicle had slowed, the ride was rough, and I could feel some serious turning and winding of the vehicle. My heart started to pound again after the little calm I had managed to muster. I felt the end was near. I started to wonder how much it would hurt, how long it would last, and how much I would bleed. How would Priya take it? How would she manage? So many thoughts began to cloud my mind. I felt like I would faint.

The vehicle slowed and then stopped. I was held by the right arm and asked to get down. I climbed down with trembling legs. My legs buckled. There was hardly any strength in them. I asked my captor if I could pee. He guided me a few steps, untied my hands and said, "Go ahead." My blindfold was still tight. I fumbled to open my zipper and managed to pee. All this while there was very little conversation between my captors. I had been straining to make something out of their conversation. Some clues, some names, some purpose but nothing. They talked very little and only about water storage, food and ammunition.

A loud command jolted me. "Let's go!" said the man whose authoritative voice marked him clearly as the leader. Another asked quietly if he should take the vehicle back, but the leader instructed him to wait. Fear surged through me— I assumed they wanted to take me farther away before shooting me.

"Wait for a while. Make sure no one's seen us, then leave," the leader continued.

A small wave of relief washed over me. Maybe they weren't planning to kill me just yet.

My hands were tied again, this time in front. I was shoved forward roughly and told to walk. Occasionally, a firm hand from behind guided me along. I realized we were ascending a moderate incline. The climb soon became harder, and I started to breathe heavily. My captors too seemed to get slower, and we got into a slow rhythmic pace. Behind me, I could hear their breaths becoming as strained as my own.

Suddenly, one of them yelled, "Be careful!" Strong hands grabbed me and guided me over some rough rocks and tangled roots. It felt like we'd been walking forever, but this endless march was oddly comforting—I found myself wishing it would never end. Each step felt like a promise of life. Though it was tough, the walking helped. Gradually, I felt a quiet sense of confidence returning. The numerous adrenaline rushes that I had experienced since my capture helped. I was calmer and less anxious now. Following the captors blindfolded, I wondered what my employer would do to get me out of the situation. They would certainly report it to the police. The big question was, what would the local police do?

Lost in my thoughts, I suddenly lost my footing and stumbled, crashing into the ground. The man behind me shouted angrily, gripping me roughly under the armpits to hoist me upright. A sharp, burning pain shot through my left ankle—I had sprained it badly on the uneven terrain. The apparent leader of the three cursed, calling me a bastard once again, his voice filled with frustration and contempt.

"Do you want us to shoot you here?" he asked in Kashmiri.

I apologized and tried to walk. It was painful, but I walked. One of the guys started to give my left side some support. It helped a lot. It seemed to me now that I might perhaps live a little longer. I wondered again about the purpose of my kidnapping. I was now almost certain that I had been kidnapped for a reason, and killing me was not the purpose, at least not in the immediate future. I was a hostage. It was a relief to think that.

The air was growing cooler. Was it the rising altitude or simply the approaching darkness? I couldn't tell. As I was thinking about it, the climb became very steep with an occasional set of rough steps that we had to negotiate. I was being constantly guided and helped now. The leader seemed anxious. He asked us to hurry up as it was getting late. Yet soon enough, their mood lightened—they began joking cheerfully about a woman from the village, clearly eager to see her later that evening. One of the guys chimed in, enthusiastically mentioning he wanted to visit her the next day. This sparked another round of laughter; it appeared this junior member had been assigned to stay behind tonight, tasked with guarding me.

By now, I was dragging my injured left foot. A few moments later, I heard a sigh of relief from one of my captors walking ahead; we'd apparently reached our destination.

We halted, and I sensed the two leaders settling down nearby. Apprehension, uncertainty and fear gripped me, and I felt a slight trembling and a chill crept up my spine. I heard a chain being dragged. Before I could react, my right ankle was chained and locked.

It was then that one of them called out loudly, "Oey Raina, relax and sit down."

So, they knew exactly who I was.

Someone untied my hands and pulled the blindfold off. I blinked rapidly, adjusting to the dimming light. For the first time, I clearly saw my masked captors. My first impressions were of a slim, short-statured guy who seemed to be responding to the commands of the burly tall fellow. The third was a more muscular and athletic looking guy. All were wearing harnesses with magazine pouches.

The athletic guy poured water into an aluminium mug from the *chaggal*, a bag-like water container, which was hanging from a wooden peg wedged into a crack in the cave wall. He handed it over to the bulky guy, who, I guessed, was the leader. The leader tipped his head back and drank the water pouring it down his throat without touching it with his lips. The athletic one followed suit. The smaller man went next, drinking in the same practiced manner. Finally, he refilled the mug and handed it to me. I drank it, trying to imitate their manner, spilling some water down my chin. The athletic guy snapped, "Don't waste it!" I wanted more but didn't dare ask.

My left ankle was swollen, and it ached.

Soon after, the trio headed down the slope. From the sound of their fading conversation, and occasional laughter, I could tell they'd moved to the right. It was likely that there was another place down the slope to where they had retired.

The Cave

I now had some time to look around. It was a wide-mouthed, deep cave with a rough, flat floor. It seemed well used. Twenty feet or so deep, it became narrow at its end. It was here that I was tied, the other end of the chain with a T end wedged into a rock slit. The chain was not a heavy one. It was like the one used by villagers to tie goats and smaller animals. It was about ten feet long, not long enough for me to move to the cave entrance ledge. While I was getting familiar with the cave, I heard someone climb up towards it. Quickly, I moved as deep as I could into the rear of the cave until I felt the rock at my back. I sat down on my haunches fearing the next moments.

The short-statured guy, still masked, came up. He had a biscuit packet in his hand. He placed it before me and said, "Eat." He also filled some water in the mug and kept it near me. From his shoulder, he threw a blanket and said, "For you".

When he was about to leave, I mumbled in my best Kashmiri that I needed to ease myself. He looked at me perplexed and told me to wait. After a while, he returned with his weapon slung on his shoulder and a few old newspaper pages. He tossed the papers towards me and stepped back a few paces, warning me not to attempt anything adventurous. Then he threw me a keychain with a single key on it. I understood he wanted me to unlock myself. I unlocked the small padlock. He unslung the weapon, which looked like an AK 47, the kind of which are displayed in the news next to the slain terrorist, he cocked it and pointing it at me, asked me to get up. I got up slowly.

"Pick up the papers", he said.

I did so. My ankle hurt, and my legs felt numb.

"Move!" he commanded and remained standing where he was while I moved towards the ledge.

On reaching it, he said "Go left".

I saw a footpath leading left, rising steeply uphill. I began to climb. About fifty feet away was a clearing – a shallow depression among the rocks, roughly twenty by fifteen feet in size. Immediately, I noticed the smell and signs of open defecation. All the while he followed me, staying about ten feet away. Upon reaching the spot, he signalled me to move forward, stepping back slightly without taking his eyes off me. I looked pleadingly at him as I started unbuckling my belt. He understood my expression and said, "Don't worry. I will only be able to see your head, nothing more." From the wrinkles around his eyes, it seemed he was smiling and enjoying the moment.

I went about my business, grateful that I could. I cleaned myself as best as I could using the paper and some earth. After buttoning up my trousers, I returned to my chain without needing instructions. When I reached the chain, he asked me to chain myself and lock it. I figured he wanted me to throw the key to him, which I did. Summoning some courage, I asked where and how I could wash my hands. This time, he responded angrily.

"This is not a hotel!", he yelled. "Use the water in the tin can if you want to," he added sharply, picking up the key before leaving.

I waited quietly to process what had happened, but my thoughts were blurred, and I was confused. I took some water from the can, did a token hand wash of my left hand, and dried it on my trousers. I opened the biscuit packet - an inexpensive, popular brand, Parle G, and began to eat.

The night was not as cold as I had anticipated, but the blanket was still inadequate. I slept on the muddy, stone floor tucking the blanket tucked around and under me for a bit of cushioning. My sleep was restless and fragmented, interrupted frequently with bouts of nightmares. Whatever little sleep I got was only because I was physically and mentally exhausted.

The Next Day

Since I was only half asleep in the wee hours, I could hear the *Azaan* in the distance and some cockerels piercing the silence. I now knew that there was a village somewhere in the distance. As I peered out, I saw the sun come up a little right of the cave opening. That must be East. So, I now knew the direction my cave was facing. I sat up trying to see more but my thoughts overtook my desire to observe. What happened yesterday? What is happening now? What was going on, and why me? These were some of the questions on my mind.

I looked at the chain, running it through my fingers to gauge if it could be cut or broken. I fiddled with the padlock, wondering if there was any chance I could open it. I was shaken from my thoughts by the sound of approaching footsteps. I shrank into my blanket pulling it over my shoulder. I watched as the junior – the one who seemed to be my permanent guard - appeared. First his head emerged, followed by his body, as he climbed onto the cave's ledge.

He was armed with the rifle slung over his right shoulder. He had a large plate called *thali* in one hand and a jug in the other. He placed the jug on the floor. He transferred the *thali* from his right hand to his left hand, unslung the rifle from his shoulder, and hung it on a wooden peg wedged in the crack in the rock. He wasn't wearing any pouch harness this time around; he was just in a *salwar* (Muslim trousers) and shirt with a sleeveless sweater. His face was, however, covered tightly with a cloth. He kept the plate in front of me, staying a few feet away. It had two *rotis*, (flat bread like wheat flour tortillas) with a little pickle on it. It was a meagre meal in a large plate for a very hungry man.

He took my tin can, threw out the little water it had, and poured some hot concoction from the jug into it. "Eat," he said, turning around immediately to retrieve his weapon before trotting down and leaving. Judging from the sound of his footsteps, I figured that he had gone to the right, somewhere behind the cave - perhaps to a log hut or some other shelter.

I started to eat and quite enjoyed the first bite of bread and pickle. The lukewarm salty concoction was unmistakeably Kashmiri *noon chai*. As I finished the meal, I felt better, and my morale improved. It felt like the right time to name my captors.

I decided to name my caretaker, 'Junaid' - so typically Kashmiri. The athletic looking one, perhaps, 'Masud,' sounded fitting. And the leader would be 'Khalid'. Of course, I wished I knew their real names. Talking to someone using his name makes it so much easier to connect with them.

I pushed the large plate away to the side, got up and tried to stretch a bit. I walked a few paces up and down as much as the chain would allow. I pulled at the chain to ascertain its robustness but did not try too hard out of fear. Nothing was happening now. I tried to go as far as I could towards the mouth of the cave many times to see what was beyond the ledge. There was nothing I could see because of my deep location in the cave.

After about an hour, I heard footsteps approaching the cave and then fading away into the distance. It seemed two of my captors had left, leaving just one behind. I wondered which one remained. This also meant that the path below the cave likely went past the base of the cave and connected the hut to the village or somewhere beyond. Unable to verify my assumptions, I lay down resignedly to rest.

Suddenly, waking up, I realized I had dozed off. Soon, sleep overtook me again – this time, though, I was aware I was drifting off. It offered some comfort; the constant mental turmoil was taking its toll.

It must have been late afternoon when I felt a gentle nudge in my ribs and woke with a start. Junaid had lightly kicked me, and my sudden reaction startled him as well, causing him to step back. He tossed a packet of Parle-G biscuits toward me and poured some water into the tin can. I told him I'd have it later. Gathering my courage, I asked Junaid what I had done to deserve this. He stared at me silently for a moment, his face still covered.

He then said, "You are our power".

I noticed that he had hung his rifle on the same wooden peg. As he picked up his rifle and prepared to leave with the lunch plate, I told him I needed to ease myself. He took the key out of his right pocket and threw it at me. I unchained myself and the ritual of yesterday followed. He stepped back.

I passed in front of him and climbed the path to the clearing while he kept watch. I had no urge except to urinate. But I took some time to look at the surrounding area. I could not see much beyond the open depression. I got up and adjusted my trousers and walked back and chained myself and threw the key back to Junaid. This time, with rifle in hand, Junaid came over to check if the lock was secure.

He was close enough for me to tackle him - if I had the guts. If I did, I would have the key to free myself and a weapon, though I had no idea how to use it. Still, I could make my escape and go to the nearest village or Police post.

But I was frozen physically, and Junaid left.

I was in for another evening and the night. I ate the entire packet of biscuits and washed them down with water. Two things were clear to me. First, I was important to my captors - or so I believed. Afterall, he had called me their "power." Second, I was in no imminent danger of being shot – a realization that brought me unexpected relief.

I began to run over the past events again but quickly abandoned this, deciding to think ahead instead, but there was nothing to think about. Soon, darkness fell. Later, hearing the distant *Azaan* again, I chose to turn in for the night. Surprisingly, my thoughts drifted to happier memories from my past, and soon I fell asleep.

I woke up during the night to urinate. I went as far as the chain would allow me and peed on some rock, like I had done a few times before. The spot and the cave had begun to stink.

An occasional gust of wind from the wide opening of the cave would freshen things up a bit. My captor who served me seemed oblivious to this, perhaps because he kept his face and nose covered when he came up to the cave. The swelling in my left ankle had subsided considerably because of reduced movement and rest. I was able to put my weight on it again without much difficulty.

I tried falling asleep again but couldn't. Scary thoughts plagued me. I was a hostage for certain, probably meant to be exchanged for something, someone or some demand. But what exactly? I wondered. It was of no use. Without an iota of an idea, even taking a wild guess felt impossible. I thought I would chat up Junaid and see what information I could gather.

Junaid arrived in the morning with two slices of bread and some tea.

"*Bhai* (brother) why am I here?", I asked.

He looked at me and merely said that I would soon know and would be free in a few days, God willing.

"*Bhai*", I began again, but he cut me short and said he hoped my employers valued my life.

He took the weapon of the hook and went down. What does my company have to do with all this? It was merely a juice packaging company. The owner was a Kashmiri Muslim. Why would the Kashmiri militants target a Kashmiri venture? Was it because other employees were not Kashmiri or Muslims, I wondered?

Junaid's remarks were intriguing and occupied my mind for the rest of the day. Evening came, and soon after the *Azaan,* Junaid bought me dinner. This time it was again two *roti*s but with a meat stew and half a raw onion. The bowl had two small pieces of meat with just enough gravy. I had no way of knowing what meat it was, and frankly, I couldn't care. Being Hindu, I was forbidden to eat beef, but this time I didn't want to know or worry about it. I relished my dinner. With the last big piece of *roti*, I carefully cleaned the bowl and finished it off, washing it down with water.

Unlike before, I did not push the *thali* away. I wanted to see how close Junaid would come to collect it. But he did not turn up that evening. I finally pushed the plate away to make space to sleep.

After sunset, I heard faint voices coming closer to the cave. I sat up to hear these more clearly. They appeared to be having an agitated argument. As they came closer to the cave, I could clearly hear one of them say in Kashmiri,

"Let us finish him and change our location."

"They won't release Tariq."

"Raina is too small a person to matter".

"It hasn't even made any headlines in any good paper".

They sounded frustrated and jumpy. The voices faded away as they went past the cave. I could not make out the conversation between the two and Junaid. Khalid and Masud had returned. My heart pounded. Soon, I heard footsteps coming up. Masud was leading, followed by Khalid and Junaid. As they came up to the cave, they covered their faces with the *Keffiyeh*. While their faces were visible for a moment, I couldn't make out much because of the low light, which was behind them. Masud came close and kicked the plate and the metal bowl away. Junaid quickly picked these up. Masud lifted me by the hair as I stood up and he slapped me.

"Worthless vermin!" he yelled in Kashmiri.

I started to weep and beg. Was this really me begging and crying? I was known for standing up to bullies in school and later in college. My seniors in college had a hard time trying to put me through the customary ragging the new students are subjected to. What had happened to my fighting spirit?

Khalid stepped up and held me by my collar and yelled, "Stop weeping like a woman you coward!"

"These Hindus are such cowards. Once they convert, they become lions," he said while shaking me.

Then, he too slapped me and asked how many Hindu employees were senior to me in our company office in Delhi. I blinked and thought for a while, keeping my left hand on my cheek to protect myself from more slaps that might follow.

"Three," I said, "but they are very senior. One is in Germany to buy equipment."

"They have fooled us," said Khalid. "They have sent a worthless chap".

Things began to become clear now. So, it was a deliberate setup by my company. My life might soon end because I wasn't a hostage of adequate value.

"*Bhai*", I mumbled, "inform my family that I would be killed. They will panic and maybe get the media involved", I said.

"We have done that," he said.

"Give them a day or two," I pleaded.

I was slapped again, and then they left, with Junaid leaving last.

Prepared to Die

My legs gave way, and I dropped on the cave floor. My time seemed to be over. I was sweating profusely. I had to do something. I pulled at the chain to see if it would give way. I examined the lock. But it was was futile.

Could I overpower Junaid? I dismissed the idea as preposterous. Should I somehow kill myself before they do? That was silly, too, because I had no means to kill myself with. I thought of my wife and two children. While Priya could work as a teacher, she wouldn't earn enough to run the family. My insurance wasn't enough either for the education of my kids. I felt anger mingled with fear. My own company had sent me in as a hostage - this realization angered me more.

It was then that my foot suddenly brushed against something at the spot where I'd urinated at night. It was a fist-sized stone, with a pointed end, though not very sharp. I grabbed it, and it seemed to fit well in my hand. I had found a weapon. I put the stone in my right pocket. Could I fight three guys with rifles with this stone? That was impossible. But I could tackle Junaid if he got close enough. But as Khalid had said, I was weak and a coward. I began to sob silently again. I was done for. Like all condemned men, I could not sleep at all.

I saw the morning glow and heard the *Azaan* and resigned to my fate. I heard footsteps again from the hut, and I knew it was time. I prayed, which I rarely do, conjuring up images of Ram, Shiv and Shirdi Baba in my mind. The steps came closer and then began to recede. They appeared to be of Masud and Khalid. They were silent. They were leaving. I sighed with some relief. Now, fighting back was the best option.

I decided to watch Junaid closely, monitor his every move and habit, and see where I could get the better of him. Soon Junaid came up with the usual biscuits and tea in a plate. I shrunk and withdrew as deep as I could into the cave. The chain was stretched taut on the floor. Junaid hung his rifle, came close and kept the plate down in front of me. He squatted on his haunches and looked into my eyes for a while without saying anything. I too remained still and said nothing. He got up and left, taking the rifle with him from the wooden peg. If this situation reoccurred, I could smash his head with the stone and hit him again and again to immobilize him. I could take the key from his pocket, steal the rifle so he can't use it and run away to the village or to a police post. A plan, however silly, had begun to form in my mind.

I began to mentally rehearse the plan. It kept me occupied. I took out the stone and held it in my hand. I swung it several times with the pointed portion protruding. I pocketed the stone again. As I thought about what I was intending to do, my body would tremble, and all my energy seemed to drain.

In the evening, Junaid came up. The plate had two *roti*s and *'Kadam',* a leafy vegetable. I said in a shaky voice that I needed to go and ease myself. He stepped back and threw the key at me. I unlocked the lock and, with trembling legs, went up to the open space which had become my toilet. I had the stone in my pocket, but the situation was not right, or so I pretended to believe. I simply could not muster up the courage to execute the plan. After spending a few more minutes pretending to ease myself, but thinking of my plan all the while, I got up and buttoned up my trousers. I came down and as per the drill that had set in, I locked my chain to my ankle and threw the key a little away but not as far as I usually did. Then, I quickly put the blanket on my right shoulder to prevent Junaid from seeing that I had put my hand in my pocket to grab the stone.

When Junaid came closer to pick up the key, I had the stone in my hand. He was close enough. He crouched to pick up the key. The moment to strike him had come. But my body failed me. I could not move my hand out of my pocket. I froze. I began trembling. Junaid picked up the key and withdrew. He sensed that something was amiss.

"Are you well?", he asked me in Kashmiri looking curiously at me.

I just shrugged and replied, "How can anyone about to die be fine?"

He lowered his eyes and left. I had lost an opportunity. I wondered if I would get another chance.

I cursed myself all night. I was slated to die. I had nothing to lose. It's best to die trying. I had to try and do something for the sake of my wife and my kids. I owed it to them. I began to psychologically condition myself. I removed the stone from my pocket and rehearsed swinging it. I repeated this exercise many times that night. I decided to die trying to escape. Why should I be shot like a dog? It was easy to think this way, but whether I could muster the courage and strength to actually do it was another matter altogether.

Dawn broke, and I heard the *Azaan*. It was probably my last day in this world. I bit myself on the left hand to check if I was alive and awake. I winced. I was awake. This was real. I waited.

The sun rose up further. I heard Junaid's footsteps. I withdrew in the cave, as much as I could, to draw Junaid within reach. This time Junaid had a plate with a bowl on it. My heart was pounding. I was breathing heavily, unable to notice anything else but Junaid and his actions in detail. He shifted the plate from his right hand to his left hand. He unslung his rifle with his right hand and hung it on the wooden peg as usual. He came up close and placed the plate in front of me. He was on his haunches.

He said in a soft voice, "I have made *Halwa* (a sweet mash of ghee, flour and water) for you today.

He had hardly finished speaking when I pulled the stone from my pocket with my right hand, grabbed Junaid's hair with my left, and swung hard, striking him on the temple. The stone found its mark.

A startled Junaid tumbled to his right trying to get up and get away. I jumped on him with the chain stretching taut and hit him hard on his head. Junaid raised his hands to his head to protect himself. A fearful frenzy gripped me, and I started hitting his head repeatedly and fast. Junaid began to groan loudly. After countless blows to his head, I felt the skull crack but continued to hit him with the same frenzy till Junaid became limp and quiet. I continued to bash his head slower but harder. I felt part of his head turn soft. Realizing that Junaid had stopped moving, I also stopped, panting heavily. I was sweating and trembling. I waited a few moments to get my breath back, and then I pulled Junaid closer. He began to move a bit, and I picked up the stone again but quickly realized that he would no longer pose a threat to me. The movement of his limbs was perhaps a precursor to his death. He convulsed a few times and was motionless. His face was uncovered now. He was a handsome young man, but he would not have prevented my murder. I pulled the key from his pocket, still trembling. With very shaky hands I unlocked the chain around my ankle. I pushed myself a few feet back with my legs and began to regain my breath and my composure.

A sense of relief and elation slowly filled me. I got up shakily. My shoulders drew back, and my chest puffed out. I had done it and was most likely free now. I walked to where the *chaggal* was and had a few gulps of water.

For the first time, I walked to the edge of the cave. The ledge overlooked the entire area to the east. I could now see for miles. I could see the track along the ridge that led up to the slope leading to the cave. The slope to the cave had a few natural steps leading to it. In the distance, perhaps two or three miles away, I could see the village. The *Azaan* that I heard every day likely came from this village. I tried to gaze north and south but couldn't see anything because of the dense trees. I spotted the track that went towards the southwest. I also noticed a small wooden hut in that direction amongst dense pines, about a hundred metres away. It took me a minute or two to absorb it all. I now wanted to get away. I was uncertain about what to do. Since I wasn't in any immediate danger anymore, I paused to think before making my escape. The village could be sympathetic to the militants, I thought, since the militants felt safe here. It may or may not have a police post. It wasn't wise to go there. I had very few options. I would have to risk going into the wilderness. While I was contemplating my next move, I noticed a lone person walking towards the cave. He may have been a mile or less away. I peered but couldn't make out much. I was fearful that one of the militants was returning to finish me off and leave the cave as they had discussed yesterday. It filled me with fear once again.

I went and grabbed Junaid's rifle. It appeared complicated. I saw the bolt with which they cock the weapon in movies. I tried to pull it back, but it would not move much. I tried again a few times without success. The guy was now about three or four hundred yards away. I began to realize that he indeed was armed. I was now beginning to get desperate and frustrated. I realized that the lever on the right side seemed to limit the movement of the bolt. I tried to shift it down, and it moved. I pulled the bolt back. This time it went all the way back since I had applied quite a force. I saw a bullet in the slot from where the metal had moved back. I left the bolt, or should I say it slipped my fingers, and the round went into the barrel. I wondered if the weapon had another safety feature. I tried to look around the cave to see if there was a place behind which I could take cover. There was none. I retreated as far back as I could into the cave, trying to keep the maximum distance between me and the cave entrance, and crouched. I was certain he would come up to the cave. I soon heard footsteps going past the cave towards the cabin.

"Rafiq, Oey Rafiq!" called the militant.

Junaid was Rafiq after all. My heart started to pound again. I put the rifle to my shoulder and recalling our shooting lessons during our school days training with Air Rifles, I aligned the tip atop the barrel end with the U on the sight nearer the eye and aimed at the place where the militant would emerge while coming up.

"Rafiq! Where are you?" shouted the militant who I thought was Masud.

He had perhaps returned alone to either shift me or kill me. My heart was pounding, I waited. I then heard footsteps coming up. My lips and throat went dry. I began to feel dizzy. But I held my stance. Then I saw a head come up. His silhouette made him stand out Then his chest and torso came into view.

Masud must have then noticed Rafiq lying in a pool of blood and he swung to get his rifle off his shoulder. I was aiming at his chest, and I pressed the trigger. Four or five shots rang out. I instinctively released the trigger, getting shocked at so many rounds being fired so quickly. I then heard Masud groan and lean towards his right, slip and fall. I remained crouched. His rifle was still in his hand, and he was trying to regain control of himself and the rifle. Spurred by panic, I swiftly moved towards him and placing the barrel near his face pulled the trigger. A few more rounds got discharged. His face became unrecognizable, and he lay still. I would never know what he looked like, or what his real name was. I again felt the same relief and a sense of elation. This time the elation was immense.

Adrenaline subsiding, I sat down exhausted. I was less afraid now. I was free and had a weapon and had used it. I would familiarize myself with it and understand it later. I also realized that this cave would draw the attention of the villagers around. Bullets had been fired twice, which would have been heard by the villagers. I should now move out quickly, in which direction was irrelevant.

I cautiously moved out, down the slope, to the track. I spotted and entered the hut with my rifle pointing towards it. There was nobody there. It had a stove and some utensils, and a pouch harness with some AK magazines, likely belonging to Rafiq, hung on a peg. Along with it, there was a plastic water bottle. There was a metallic trunk box, dented with time and misuse. I opened it and discovered a walkie talkie and an old military grade binoculars. Under these, there were a few clothes, a *salwar* and some shirts. I pulled out one pair. Further rummaging through the box, I found a bundle of cash. There were maybe a few thousand rupees, which I pocketed. I looked around to see if my watch, which they had taken from me, was also in the box.

I thought about how much time I had before the villagers reported the matter to the local police, which I knew was heavily compromised and full of militant sympathizers. They could also inform the militants about the fire they had heard. How long would it take for them to come and investigate? I gave myself an hour, during which time I had to put maximum distance between myself and the cave. I noticed two relatively clean blankets on the single cot. I threw the pair of *salwar* and shirt on the blankets, rolled these up and tied them in a bundle by tearing a bed sheet. I then pulled down Rafiq's pouch harness. It had two magazines in it. I thought of going up and collecting Masud's rifle and magazines as well.

I cautiously looked out and went up the cave again to where Masud lay bleeding and dead. One look at his harness revealed that two magazines were badly damaged by the first set of bullets I had fired from twenty feet or so away. I could only retrieve one magazine of the three he was carrying. The fourth one was on the weapon, which I grabbed and went down. I put the retrieved magazine in Rafiq's pouch. I loosely wore the harness and swung the blanket around my shoulder. I took the water bottle and the binoculars. I felt I had no use for the Walkie Talkie so left it there, a decision I would regret later.

Heavily laden I went out of the hut. I stopped to think which way I should go. There was a path leading to the Southwest and away from the cave. It was likely being used by militants. So, I decided to go north on untrodden ground, amongst the pine trees. It would lead me to the area overlooking the village, east of the cave. The pine needles made it difficult for me to walk with my city shoes, which had almost smooth soles. If it was difficult for me, it would perhaps be difficult for others as well, if they tried to follow me.

I must have walked for about an hour, gaining some height when I started to feel exhausted. My ankle, which I thought was healing, began to hurt again. I sat down and looked around. There were trees surrounding me, and I could not see beyond fifty yards or so. I needed to survey the area around me. I stood and began trudging up. Most times, I walked up the slope to gain height and then, sometimes, I walked along the contour to ease my efforts. I was getting away and gaining a bit of height at the same time.

About fifteen minutes into my slippery trek over pine needles, I came across a small clearing. It was quite flat and about ten feet in diameter, with young pine trees around that were roughly four or five feet tall. From here, I could see the entire village in the distance and the terrain around, along with the opening of the cave where I had been held captive. I put my gear down and decided to take a rest. I opened the half-empty bottle and drank sparingly, knowing there was little water left that I must keep for later. It must have been noon by now.

The sun was directly overhead. The morning had seen much action. I was free, yet a runaway hostage of the militants. I lay down, shielding my eyes from the sun with my arm, and dozed off for a while.

I woke up, sensing that I might still be in danger. The sun had shifted further west. I may have slept for about an hour. Sitting up, I could see nothing. This also meant that no one could see me until they reached the spot. I peered, stretching my neck, but to no avail. I decided to stand up and look around.

As soon as I stood, I noticed a grey police vehicle in the distance, parked about half a mile from the cave. I fumbled for the binoculars among the gear that was scattered around. Once I found them, I focused and looked through the binoculars, clearly seeing that it was indeed a police vehicle with four policemen pointing towards the cave. Perhaps the police knew about the cave. It was odd that they weren't approaching it. Perhaps they were being cautious. Some villagers had gathered about half a mile away from the vehicle, curious and cautious onlookers - so very typical of India.

As I continued to peer towards the village, I noticed a convoy of four military green vehicles approaching, raising dust in their wake. I realized there was no road to the village, only a track. Looking through the binoculars again, I spotted an open light vehicle with a kind of machine gun mounted on it, followed by another light vehicle. The third was a light truck, followed again by a vehicle like the leading one, also with a machine gun. This convoy soon passed the village and the curious crowd, reaching the police vehicle and stopping. About fifteen or twenty troopers disembarked and spread out in a protective cordon. I peered again and saw a policeman pointing towards the cave and engaged in an intense discussion. I also recognized the military vehicles; they were Suzuki Gypsy, a model used by the Indian Army. I couldn't identify the truck, though. Curious, I began to enjoy the scene.

After a while, the military troopers formed two teams. The smaller team began to lead while the larger team followed. Two *khaki*-clad policemen trailed behind, maintaining a safe distance from the army personnel. They were all wearing some sort of bulletproof vests and odd-looking round headgear. Their pace slowed as they approached the climb to the cave. Then, they all crouched and moved one by one. I saw a soldier trying to peer into the entrance of the cave. I heard faint orders being given by one of the men, perhaps their commander. Then, I heard a few rounds fired in automatic mode, similar to how I had fired. Silence fell again. I then saw the soldiers advancing one by one towards the cave opening. Their progress was very slow and cautious.

Suddenly, someone yelled, and all the soldiers, including the policemen, hit the ground and took cover. There was more shouting, which I couldn't make out due to the distance. I saw a soldier approach the entrance of the cave; he froze and began speaking, trying to explain the situation. The second soldier joined him, taking up a position just short of the entrance. Gradually, the second military team rose and started advancing with their rifles ready. They passed the crouching first team and halted just shy of the entrance. They then lowered their weapons and entered the cave. The two *khaki*-clad policemen also got up from their crouched positions but remained where they were. The commander, along with a few soldiers, cautiously approached the hut. I couldn't see beyond the entrance of the cave, so I didn't know what was happening inside. Soon, conversations began in the area. The *khaki*-clad policemen bravely joined the military now. I saw the commander talking on some sort of wireless radio.

I felt proud of myself, thinking I had inadvertently contributed to the national effort. I wondered whether I should leave my hideout and join the army, revealing my identity. But their cautiousness made me reconsider. I could be shot before they even knew who I was.

At this point, another military convoy of four vehicles was approaching the site, moving considerably faster. They arrived about ten minutes later. I saw a lot of saluting and handshakes. Perhaps the army detachment was claiming credit for the militants killed. Soon, the village crowd began moving towards the cave. The military and police, who had now joined with their vehicles, held them back. I watched as both bodies were retrieved and taken to the truck. There was a lot of cheering and sloganeering. One of the soldiers was taking photos. Then some soldiers went towards the hut again and returned with various items, including a metal box trunk. It was getting dark. The first group of four vehicles left, followed by the second group about fifteen minutes later. During this time, the policemen were scouring the site, taking notes. A surge of civilians then entered the cave. It all seemed quite festive. As the sun set, the villagers began returning to their homes. I had missed my chance to reach safety. I decided to spend the night in this secure place. A little while later, I heard the *Azaan*. It had been a long, harrowing, and violent day that had drained me in ways I could hardly imagine. I took another sip of water and prepared to sleep. I spread one blanket under me and took the other over me. I don't know how long I stayed awake or when I finally fell asleep.

I heard a rustling in the trees and woke up with a start. I looked around, but I couldn't see anything. Perhaps a fox was investigating the area. I wasn't fully awake, though. The half-moon lit the surroundings, and it seemed to be around 3 AM. I missed my watch terribly. Soon, I slipped back into sleep and was roused by the sound of birds chirping. It was another dawn, and I had begun to lose track of the days.

I got up and walked some distance away from my spot to relieve myself, facing the direction of the cave. As the light grew brighter, I noticed four men walking along the path that led to the cave. I went back to grab my binoculars to get a better look. They were militants moving urgently toward the cave. All four entered it, but they soon emerged and headed toward the hut before disappearing from sight. I was merely an hour or so away from them. My only advantage was that they had no idea which direction I had taken. I started to gather my belongings and organize them for easier carry. Having done that as best as I could, I tried to observe the area around the cave once more. The four had split into two teams. Two of them were heading south along the path, while the other two came directly toward me over the same area I had traversed. They were occasionally talking on their walkie-talkies. If I had taken the radio set from the cabin, I would have known what they were up to. I felt a surge of panic. I hastily put on my harness and gathered my gear. I swung both weapons over my right shoulder and began to climb.

The sun was rising on the horizon, and I was moving away from it toward the west. Soon, I was breathless and panting. I slowed my pace to catch my breath, settling into a slow, rhythmic walk as I wove through the trees, occasionally slipping on the pine needles. This gradual pace wasn't tiring me anymore.

I must have walked for about two hours or more, judging by the sun's position. I was convinced that I wasn't being followed anymore. My reasoning was simple: my captors would think that if I had escaped, I would head to the nearby village to seek local help. They wouldn't have imagined that I would eliminate two of their colleagues before making my escape. They would likely assume that someone in the village had tipped off the army. They would believe the army was responsible for killing the two militants. They would have no idea that I had their weapons with me. They would assume that the army took these away when clearing out the hideout. All these thoughts offered me a sense of safety.

At this point, I began to feel a bit dizzy and breathless again. I felt lightheaded and somewhat uncomfortable. Perhaps I had gained some altitude, and the air was thinner. I finally stopped and sat down to rest, then lay back against the slope. I closed my eyes and dozed off. It must have only been a few minutes when I woke up. The sun was still where I had left it. I collected my things and got up to move on. I stood gazing here and there wondering where to go next. It felt like an aimless escape. Nevertheless, I continued up the slope. After about an hour of climbing, I noticed that the trees were becoming sparse. The sun peeked onto wider spaces now and for longer durations between shadows. I noticed a vast, gradual, undulating grassy expanse just above the tree line. This must be the summer pastureland of the *Gujjar*s, called *Bhaikh*s.

*Gujjar*s are a nomadic tribe who move up into the mountains with their herds in summer and come down to the plains during winter months. Their grazing areas are referred to as *Bhaikh*s.

I stopped short, well within the tree line, and could now hear a trickle of water somewhere. I discerned the possible direction and walked towards it. From a wet, moss-infested rock, a steady trickle of water flowed down to a small puddle the size of a medium tub. It was overflowing, and the water ran down the slope to a grassy area nourished by the flow. I had stumbled upon a mountainous oasis of sorts. There was a small clearing next to it, perhaps about ten feet away, with ample sunlight streaming down on the patch. It was just enough to accommodate the items I was carrying. I decided to camp here for the rest of the day and night. I filled my water bottle, took a drink, and then refilled it and capped it. I then shifted my gear to the clearing. I didn't sit to rest but instead took off my clothes and washed myself, feeling so refreshed. I also cleaned my clothes as best as I could and spread them out to dry. Naked, I now felt cold. I opened the blanket bundle, took out the *Salwar* and *Kameez* (shirt), and put them on, still feeling a little chilly. I wrapped a blanket around myself and felt the pangs of hunger. I hadn't eaten for over 36 hours. The last meal I 'saw' was the *Halwa* prepared by Rafiq. I wished I had eaten some then or at least carried some along. I could think like this now because I felt relatively safe and in control of the situation. A few hours earlier, I had been a meek guy scurrying away from danger as fast as I could.

It was time to check out and learn more about the rifles I carried. I first picked up Rafiq's rifle, the one with which I had done all the shooting. I examined the magazine and fiddled with a small catch under the rifle and behind the magazine. It came loose. I pulled it out. It still had rounds in it. Then I pulled the cocking lever, and another round popped out. What if it had accidentally fired while I was escaping? A chill went down my spine thinking of what could have happened. I started to remove the remaining rounds from the magazine. There were twelve rounds. I pulled the cocking lever once more to make sure there were no more rounds in the rifle. There seemed to be none. The hole where the round goes into the barrel was empty. Next, I checked the lever on the right, which had initially hampered the movement of the bolt. It had three positions: the top position appeared to be the safety, the middle for automatic fire, and the last for single fire. Did one have to cock it every time a single round was fired? I wondered. I put the bullets back into the magazine through trial and error. I was about to place it back in the rifle but decided to insert one from the pouch instead. This one was heavier and likely full. I didn't know how many rounds it contained. I managed to insert the new magazine without much difficulty; it was simple. The sun had shifted from over the drying clothes, so I adjusted them under the sunlight again. I now understood the rudimentary operation of an AK rifle. This much training was enough for today. I began to think of food and felt miserable. I drank some more water. I went back to the pond to refill the water bottle. I saw my reflection in the pond. I was dishevelled and could have mistaken myself for a militant. After filling the water, I returned and picked up my shirt and undergarments, which were nearly dry, but my trousers were still damp. The sun was setting now. I took my rifle and binoculars and walked about fifty paces to the end of the tree line. While remaining in the shadows of the trees, I first peered at the landscape. I thought I spotted a wisp of smoke in the distance to my left. It must be west, I thought, two or three miles away. Should I head out now to seek some food? I could pay for it. I estimated it would take me an hour or more. It would be dark by then, and I didn't know what I would encounter en route. So, I decided against it. I planned to leave very early the next morning and look at the spot from a closer distance before deciding on a course of action. I would have to endure the hunger tonight.

I had a restless night, waking up every now and then to check the time. The moon was up, but I wasn't an expert at telling the time based on its position. At some point, I decided to pack up and move toward the smoke. The moonlight helped me gather my things, and I slung them over both shoulders as I ventured out onto the grassy ground, staying close to the tree line in case I needed cover. I must have walked for about an hour when dawn broke, and I was quickly able to see much farther. I noticed puffs of smoke about a mile away, along with a gradual rise ahead. I approached it cautiously while keeping myself close to the tree line. I started to walk slowly up the slope and the moment I was able to see across the rise, I froze. To anyone observing the slope, they would have only seen my head emerge. A small target from a distance. About three hundred yards away, I spotted the smoke and the hut it was rising from. I lay low to reduce my silhouette. I was becoming tactical already. Through my binoculars, I could see it was a *Gujjar* hut. *Gujjar*s, or *Bakarwaal* as they are sometimes called, are nomadic tribes of grazers who move to higher altitudes in summer to graze their animals and descend to lower altitudes in winter. They build one or two shelters with logs in their traditional grazing areas. These logs are placed horizontally, resting on one side of a hill slope. These logs make the roof. Vertical logs support all other sides, like walls, creating a sort of shelter. It is usually left open and unguarded in winter, and all their belongings are transported away by ponies.

I observed a family of four going about their business: a tall man with a beard, two women, and a young lad. There were goats, sheep, and a few ponies grazing on the gently undulating, lush grassy *Bhaikhs*. I waited and watched for a while. It seemed safe unless they surprised me by pulling out a gun or rifle. I tried to make myself as intimidating as possible. I considered covering my face but decided against it because I had nothing to cover it with. I slung my spare rifle and everything else over my left shoulder while holding one rifle in my right hand. In case of a confrontation, I would throw all my belongings, hit the ground to present a smaller target, cock my rifle, and fire back. See, I was almost a trained militant myself, and that too in just two days. I checked the safety and switched it to single fire, which I had not yet tested.

I started to walk towards the hut as the sun rose behind me. About a hundred yards away, the family noticed me. I saw the woman push the younger woman towards the hut, gesturing for her to go in. The other three stood still, looking at me as I approached them. When I was about thirty yards away, I waved to them. The bearded man and the young lad both waved back. As I got closer, the bearded man walked up and extended his hand. I shifted my rifle to my left hand, shook his hand, and stepped sideways while moving my rifle back to my right hand. He began to welcome me in Gujjari, a mix of Punjabi, Pahari (mountain dweller's language), and Pothohari, which is spoken on the Pakistan side of Kashmir. I understood most of it. The first thing I said to them in Kashmiri was that I was hungry. They seemed to understand, and a flurry of activity ensued. A bundle of blankets was placed on a log outside the hut for me to sit on. I laid my belongings, including the spare rifle, on the ground. The boy approached with a curious expression. I gestured for him to stay away, and he took a few steps back. He must have been fifteen or sixteen—fairly tall for his age and very athletic. The older woman went inside the hut and soon came back with a metallic tumbler wrapped in a piece of cloth. I took the tumbler from her and had my first sip of something hot. It was sweet hot milk. I took another sip, and it felt heavenly indeed. As the milk cooled, I started taking bigger gulps. No one spoke but continued to look at me with awe. Then the woman said, "I will get you some *roti*s." I smiled and nodded. She quickly ran back into the hut, seemingly giving instructions to the young woman. The girl responded to her mother's instructions in a wonderfully soft voice, and I was almost mesmerized by it. The *Gujjar* or *Bakarwaal*, whoever he was, mistook me for a militant and said that '*Fauji*' (Army men) sometimes come here. I realized he wanted to get rid of me as quickly as possible. I nodded. I asked him if he had a '*bandook*' (gun).

"Yes," he replied.

"Bring it out and show it to me," I ordered.

He went inside. Keeping the half-empty glass on the ground, I picked up the rifle. The young boy seemed alarmed. The older man, perhaps in his late forties, came out with an old single-barrel shotgun.

I gestured to him, and he went back into the hut. He returned shortly, empty-handed. I leaned my rifle against the log I was sitting on, picked up the tumbler, and drained the remaining milk in one go. The boy came forward and took the metallic tumbler from my hand. The man tried to strike a conversation with me.

"Where are you headed?" he asked.

"Sopore," I replied without thinking.

After all, that was where my ordeal had begun. He mentioned it was quite a distance, and the route was infested with military presence. I nodded and said nothing.

The older lady emerged with a plate holding two *roti*s and a generous dollop of white butter. The butter had begun to melt. I accepted the plate from her and placed it on my lap. I broke off a morsel, dipped it in the butter, and took my first bite of solid food in a while. The *roti* was mildly salty with chili flakes. It was possibly the tastiest bite I had ever had. The younger lady then came out, leaning against one of the log walls of the hut, holding another *roti* on a plate. She appeared to be about twenty, a tall and athletic young girl. She had rolled up her shirt sleeves, likely while cooking the *rotis* over an open fire. Her skin was heavily tanned, as I could see the difference in the complexion of her arms. She had sharp features and striking eyes set wide apart. She was a beauty. The mother noticed my glance at her and took the plate from her, instructing her to go back inside and make some tea for everyone. I watched her return to the hut rather reluctantly, or so I imagined. I was offered another *roti*, which I declined. My appetite seemed to have diminished over the past four or five days.

It was my turn to ask some questions. I pretended to be new in the area. I asked them if there were some villages nearby. They pointed out two. One was in the direction from where I thought I had come, and another was further south. The one I seemed to have come from, he said, was Tangpora, and the one in the South was Shatmulla. Not that the names mattered, but it was good to know.

"Does the Army come here often?" I asked.

"No, not very often", he answered.

I was disappointed to hear this since I wanted to seek the Army's protection and return to my normal life.

"If they spot you here with us, they will shoot you first and interrogate us later", he continued. "One of the family would surely be arrested and taken away for harbouring a militant", he added.

He was trying to tell me that the Army was jumpy and did not take chances. He was also conveying that I was putting their family at risk and that I had better leave soon.

"I will leave soon", I assured him in Kashmiri.

The older man seemed to understand, smiled, and folded his hands in gratitude, and as a request.

"Can you please make some more *rotis* for me to carry", I asked.

He was keen to do that and conveyed it loudly to the lady who had now gone back into the hut. The lady came out again, this time with two teacups. I asked the older man to sit with me on the log. We both took our cups and began to sip the tea. I asked the man his name. He hesitated. I told him to forget it. He seemed relieved. I asked him if I could rest in the hut until the *rotis* were made. He was more than happy. I finished the tea, and the young boy guided me inside. The young woman was at the open fire making more *rotis* for me to carry.

Suddenly, the young boy mentioned he knew how to use a *Kalashnikov*. I showed surprise and awe. He said he could strip it apart and assemble it back.

I thought for a moment and said, "Let's see you do it!"

He quickly pulled out a cotton mat used for sleeping on, called *dari* in most parts of India. I removed the magazine from the spare AK I was carrying and handed it to him, while I held the one with me closely. He placed the rifle on the rug and removed its cover, taking off the spring, bolt, and top wooden stock. Occasionally, he seemed unsure and struggled a bit. He mentioned it had been a while since he learned it. He said he would make a good militant if he was allowed by his *abba* (father). Since he was the only son, his father wouldn't permit it. He said he wished he had more brothers. He then went to where the shotgun was hung. I became apprehensive. He picked up an oily rag lying underneath the gun, applied some oil from a small glass bottle onto the cloth, and returned to oil most parts of the disassembled rifle. He assembled the weapon, fumbling occasionally. Finally, he cocked the weapon a few times and released the trigger. I was impressed. I clapped gently and smiled without speaking. He was very proud of himself. I, too, was very thankful to him for giving me my second lesson about the AK rifle.

The boy then said, "You know it's not safe for you to carry your Kalashnikov with the safety off."

"I need to be ready all the time," I replied.

He had observed the safety position on my rifle. He mentioned that the militants who taught him all of this last year even allowed him to fire. He had fired a few '*kartoos*' (rounds) in both burst and single-shot modes.

"So, you know what *burst fire* is," I asked.

"Yes," he responded, mimicking it for me.

He imitated a single shot fire for me. Tak, Tak, Tak. I now understood that a single shot did not require re-cocking; it was semi-automatic. My third lesson of the day.

My packed meal was ready in a cloth bundle. The older lady informed me that she had included some mutton pickles with it. The younger lady softly mentioned that she had refilled my water bottle with fresh water. I smiled at her and said, "*Shukriya*" (thank you). She smiled meekly while her mother glared at her. I then asked for an old pan to brew some tea. The young woman quickly picked one up from the ground and handed it to me. It was a battered aluminium pan without a handle. There was an inch-long metal strip where the handle should have been. I asked if they could spare some tea leaves and sugar. Both the mother and daughter became busy and soon I had two small pouches filled with tea leaves and sugar. They also provided some milk in a plastic bottle. The daughter then pulled out a cloth bag with carrying loops known as *thela*. She deftly packed the pan with tea, and sugar pouches and placed the packed pan in the *thela*, along with the food. I noticed that she added something tiny to the bag. I handed my clothes to her without a word. She adjusted the items, packed those as well, and handed me the bag to carry. She smiled again, and so did I. This time, sensing my departure, the mother smiled too. I peeled off two five-hundred-rupee notes and placed them on a small spice box next to the open fire stove called "*Daambur*" in rural Kashmir. The mother objected and tried to return the money. Hearing the commotion, the older man entered and joined in the refusal.

"Should I leave everything here?" I complained in broken Pahari.

It silenced them. I asked the boy to accompany me to the tree line. I didn't want to risk being fired upon from behind, even by a shotgun. He began to lead, and I followed. Near the tree line, I asked the boy to go back. I turned around and saw the three of them watching me. I waved at them, and they waved back. The young girl waved too. I saw her take the edge of her *dupatta* (a kind of large scarf worn by most Kashmiri women) to her eyes. She may have thought I would not be alive for long. It was a very touching sentiment. I reached the tree line and continued deeper into the trees before deciding on a direction. I didn't want anyone to know which way I had gone.

I turned south again. I decided to descend along a slope. It was at lower altitudes that I was likely to find a track, a road, or a village. I needed to reach some inhabited place to contact the police or the military. After about a two-hour walk and having lost some elevation, I found myself in a small clearing once more. Not more than twenty by thirty yards, it featured a dilapidated *Gujjar* hut at its edge. Next to the hut was a trickling spring with water draining into the trees. I had found an ideal resting spot. I peeped into the hut. It was empty except for a c*hullah* (open hearth) with some firewood next to it.

I unloaded my burden, placing all the weight I had been carrying next to the log wall of the hut. I walked up to the spring, splashed some water on my face, and wiped it clean with my hands. The water was cold but felt so refreshing. I then cupped my hands and took a few sips; the water was like nectar. It must have been past noon by now, and I felt hungry. I retrieved the dented container and filled it with water, drinking some before taking the rest to the fireplace. I thought of brewing some tea but needed to light the fire and had no means to do so. So, I decided to have some food and started to unpack the cloth bag. While doing so, I noticed something small fall. It was a matchbox that the young lady had so thoughtfully packed. I couldn't help but smile; what a remarkable young woman she was. I forgot about the food for a while and lit the earthen hearth. The fire crackled as I added more wood, and then I carefully placed the pan on the fire.

I opened the food packet, which contained six *rotis*. There was some pickled mutton between the layers of *rotis*. I pulled out two, added some pickles, and began to eat. I wished I had borrowed a plate as well. The pickle was delicious, and I enjoyed my meal. Hunger is the best sauce. After the meal, I clapped my hands to clean off the leftover crumbs and started to watch the water boil. I added the tea leaves, a bit of sugar, and finally some milk. My tea was ready. I removed the pan from the heat using the end of my flowing shirt. I closed the milk bottle tightly and walked to the spring, placing it in the cold water to keep the milk from curdling. I drank the tea leisurely. It was a lovely meal, and the tea was very refreshing. I spread a blanket on the flat ground and lay down for a well-deserved rest.

I decided to spend the night here. Much-needed rest, food, and respite from imminent danger rejuvenated me immensely. My ankle seemed less bothersome now. I had lost count of the days and didn't want to recount them. Perhaps it had been a week. Now that I had some time to think, I felt deeply ashamed of my behaviour during the first two days. I had acted like a coward, weeping like a frightened child. I even begged. I could have carried myself in a more dignified manner. I was always thinking of Rohan and Rhea and wanted to live for them. What if I had died in some accident? They would have moved on somehow. Priya was there for them. Then why did I act in such a deplorable way? Self-loathing consumed me. I could still be killed like I killed those two militants. Thinking of the militants, I felt no remorse for what I had done. It filled me with a sense of elation and control. Something else had changed within me. I found myself drawn to the smell of gunpowder and blood in the cave. I couldn't explain this to myself. Perhaps it was the adrenaline again. I was no longer averse to violence.

At dawn, I heard the *Azaan* again, very faint and distant. I packed my belongings for easier transport as best as I could. The pan I had carried was making too much noise, so I decided to discard it here after brewing some tea before I departed. I had two *rotis* and some pickles with me that I planned to eat later in the morning. I looked at the hut and the surrounding area with fondness one last time. It had been the best shelter in the past few days. Now, I needed to move on to reach some government authorities to get back home.

I began to descend the slope once more. After about an hour or so, I decided to take a break and enjoy my last two *rotis* for breakfast. While I ate, I heard a distant vehicle horn twice, about two miles away. My spirits lifted. I considered heading to the road to make my way to the nearest police station or a military base, hoping that then my ordeal would be over. I finished my meal and washed it down with some water. I should have been in a hurry, but I wasn't. I can't explain why I felt this way. Perhaps I had begun to relish being the solitary king of the forest and mountains. I had started to appreciate and enjoy the land my ancestors had left behind long ago.

After lounging around for about an hour, I gathered my gear, including the two rifles, and began my descent once more. I may have descended for roughly half an hour when I suddenly heard gunfire—small bursts coming from multiple directions. I froze and quickly took cover behind a large tree with an impressive girth. I was unsure which side I needed to take cover from.

I swiftly and calmly unloaded my gear, and, taking one of the rifles, cocked it to a single round mode to conserve ammunition in case I found myself in a firefight. I needed my magazine to last throughout the encounter. I could simply push the safety lever further up for burst or multi-round options. Though I felt scared again, there was a boy scout's thrill for adventure coursing through me.

The gunfire sounded about a hundred yards away or less. I positioned myself behind the tree and peered from the right side, rifle poised to fire. I could see nothing. I could also hear intermittent gunfire in the distance. The firing originated approximately a hundred yards away, while another, much fainter sound of gunfire came from about two or three hundred yards further. I began to contemplate escaping from the site up the slope once more. It seemed the best option.

What if there were more militants or the military in the area? I would be singled out and shot. Driven by curiosity, I moved from one tree to another for about fifty yards, occasionally slipping on the pine needles. Then I spotted them. There were four militants in two pairs, firing into the slope below. They were well concealed and had ample cover from the trees. Their fire was being returned, but quite inaccurately, from the lower slope, which appeared to be convex. This might have provided some protection to whoever was returning fire from afar and below. Most likely, it was the army, who had either been surprised or caught off guard while patrolling the area. The fire was so off-target that it struck trees nowhere near the militants. Perhaps encouraged by this inaccurate fire, the militants were urging each other in Kashmiri and attempting to shift to more advantageous firing positions. I now felt anxious that I had come too close. If I turned and started to climb back again, slipping over the pine needles, I might be seen and shot.

What if I joined the firefight? My fire would be drowned out by theirs and wouldn't be noticed by either side. I could even eliminate or reduce the threat to myself and perhaps to the unfortunate soldiers pinned down below. I crouched and aimed at the back of the militant closest to me, perhaps fifty or sixty yards away, and fired a single round. It missed. I saw some pine needles kicked up about two feet short of the militant. I aimed again, this time for his head. The head, however, was far from steady. I decided to aim at the upper back instead. I fired and heard a loud yell of pain from the militant as he fell forward and writhed in agony.

Another militant, about ten or fifteen yards away from the injured, said, "Hold on!", in Kashmiri and began to crawl towards him. I felt my heart pounding as I waited with the aimed rifle at the guy I had hit. The moment the other militant reached the injured one, he noticed the wound in the back while holding the injured militant. He realized that the shot had been fired from the rear. He nervously scanned the area I had taken cover in.

I moved the safety lever up a notch and aimed. The other militant noticed me. He looked shocked. Before he could drop the injured person and grab his weapon, I released a long burst at the two—maybe ten or fifteen rounds.

I watched them both slump, convulsing and making gasping sounds.

The other two glanced over their shoulders and dashed from the site into the trees. Silence fell on this side, while sporadic gunfire could still be heard from a distance. I waited for maybe three minutes. I decided to head up the slope again, knowing that if I encountered the military, I would likely be mistaken for a militant. I needed to buy time to gather my things and keep the military at bay for a little longer.

So, I cautiously moved near the still-breathing militants, tree by tree and having got close enough I fired four or five rounds into them just to make sure and ease their misery. No sooner had I fired, than I heard a volley of fire from the distance. This would have made the other two militants run faster and away, not knowing what had happened and what was happening. I moved back and replaced the magazine with a full one, hauled my stuff up and started trudging up the slope again. The sound of the fire from a distance was still audible, but its intensity had reduced. Perhaps it was a cautionary fire by the military patrol now.

I began to ascend the slope again, heading south. This direction offered the best chance of encountering habitation in the lower reaches. I trudged upward, gaining elevation.

Approximately half an hour into my climb, I could faintly hear slogans and shouts behind me.

'*Bharat Mata ki Jai*' (Glory to the Motherland),

'*Har Har Mahadev*' (Glory to Lord Shiva)

It appeared that the military had discovered the bodies of the terrorists and was celebrating 'their' kills. It was reassuring that someone else was taking credit for my actions. This relieved me of the weight of the legal or illegal acts I was committing.

I continued my climb for about three hours. I again reached a point where tree line was diminishing and open grassland of the *Bhaikh*s meadows came into view. Hugging the tree line, I began to move further Southward. Soon I spotted another *Gujjar* hut. I peered through my binoculars and saw a family of three. An old couple and a woman. Their livestock was grazing happily on the rich grass. I continued along the sparse tree line till I was near the hut. Their dog started barking and came charging toward me. I emerged from the tree line, and the dog kept its distance, seeing something in my hand. The family noticed me and, shocked by my appearance, froze. I waved to them in the friendliest manner I could muster. The old man responded, seeming to welcome me, although I knew I was most unwelcome. He called back the dog. It was well past noon, and I was hungry, so I asked the old man if I could get something to eat. He called out some instructions in *Gujjari* to the younger woman, who looked to be in her early forties. I put down my gear next to a log wall and, holding my rifle, sat down with my back against the wall, scanning the area for anything unusual. The woman went inside and returned with some lukewarm sweet milk, which I drank with relish. She then spoke in a somewhat rough voice, distorted by decades of herding animals loudly.

"I will prepare a hot meal for you," she said.

I can't quite describe it, but her words stirred something within me. Despite her unkempt clothes and the sweat-soaked odour surrounding her, she seemed quite desirable. I smiled at her without saying a word. She glanced around to see if anyone had noticed and then smiled back mildly. She went back inside, and the old man moved closer to me. I pulled the weapon closer, prompting him to stop advancing. He sat on his haunches and asked if I had been involved in the encounter with the military about two hours earlier, as they could hear faint gunfire here. I nodded. He inquired if I had lost any comrades. I nodded again, raising two fingers to indicate the number, and replied, "two" in Kashmiri. He clicked his tongue in despair and cursed the military. Perhaps he would have cursed the militants had the military been present. He then asked me about the village I belonged to. After a moment of thought, I blurted out, "Tangpora." Not wanting to answer any more questions, I closed my eyes. He understood and went to where the old lady was herding some goats to a better pasture.

I heard some pots and pans inside the *Gujjar* hut, and soon I had a plate with two *rotis* and some *daal* (lentils) in a small metallic bowl. It also contained an onion cut in half. I took the plate from her and, keeping it in my lap, began to eat. The woman went inside again and brought a metal tumbler of buttermilk. I thanked her and smiled. She went back in and, after a while, returned with two more *rotis*. I declined them. She then sat down next to me, putting the extra *rotis* aside. She wiped the sweat from her face with the *dupatta*. She was tanned and attractive in a strange way. Perhaps she sensed my thoughts, as she repeated the question the old man had asked me about our encounter. I gave her the same reply.

"You must be very tired and tense?", she asked in *Gujjari*.

"Yes," I answered, while eating, taking some gulps of buttermilk.

It was refreshing. She then suggested that I rest, and I agreed; I needed it. She got up and walked over to the old couple, who were about fifty or sixty yards away. After a brief discussion, she returned. She picked up some of my things and took them in. I followed her with the rest and my weapons. I asked her name, and she promptly replied, "Fatima."

Fatima, I repeated in my mind. From her quick, unhesitant response, I assumed that she had given her correct name.

"Do you have children?" I asked.

"Yes, I have a daughter who is married and an 18-year-old son who has gone to Baramulla to apply for a job as a policeman," she replied. "I lost my husband four years ago," she continued, sounding quite frank.

While putting away my things, she came quite close to me, brushing against me occasionally.

I mustered some courage and said, "You are very beautiful."

She slapped my face lightly, smiling and holding one corner of her *dupatta* in her teeth as if to hide her smile behind it.

"It's up to you," I said gently.

She hugged me and mentioned that it had been four long years. While holding her lightly around the waist, I asked about her in-laws. She said they were keeping an eye out for the military. One thing led to another. It was a frenzied act. I spent some of the best minutes of my life intertwined with her. She too may have felt good. I was exhausted. She adjusted her clothes and walked out, and I slept like a baby for a few hours.

When I woke up, the sun had set, and Fatima was all washed up and had changed into much fresher clothes. There was a smell of chicken being prepared. The dog must be having a treat outside somewhere too. The old man asked me if I would like some liquor or *daaru* as it's called in local parlance. I nodded, and he took out a half-filled bottle of rum. A closer look revealed it was from some military concession store. So, the military had been visiting him too. This made things precarious for me as a perceived militant.

The old man poured a miserly drink for me, added some water, and handed me the brass tumbler. He poured a similar drink for himself, said some prayers, and gulped down the drink in one go. I gulped down the drink likewise. He began to pour me another drink, but I put a hand on my tumbler, indicating that I didn't want any more. He pretended to insist but poured himself another one and drank it again in one go. We were served watery chicken and *rotis*. As night fell, I was given a spot next to the *daambur chullah* for additional warmth. The rest of the family prepared to sleep a little further away. Fatima was the farthest. Fatima and I exchanged knowing glances, but I could not engage with her any further. I asked the old man if I could get some tea before sunrise so I could leave early. He passed this on to Fatima.

I had another restless night. My thoughts and dreams drifted from the encounter site to lovely Fatima, but I managed to sleep in spells. It was still dark outside, when I heard pots and pans clattering and some activity. I got up and asked the old man for a water container for cleaning. He handed me a battered aluminium one. I filled it with water from the half-empty drum outside for the animals and headed down into some bushes about thirty yards away. After easing and cleaning myself, I returned to the hut. The old man was ready with a bar of soap and a steel jug full of water. I soaped and washed my hands while he poured the water. I shook my hands dry and wiped the excess water off onto my clothes. Dawn was now breaking.

Fatima brought out a hot brass tumbler, holding it in a cloth napkin. She extended it to me. It contained milky sweet tea. She also had a plate of some thick savoury cookies, locally called *mathee*. I relished the hot tea and some *mathee* biscuits. I pulled money from my side shirt pocket and handed a thousand rupees to the old man. He accepted it gladly and offered me a toothless smile as thanks. I looked at Fatima one last time and asked her for a white rag or a piece of cloth. She went inside and brought me her old white *dupatta*. I slung my belongings and the spare rifle over my left shoulder, picked up the other rifle with my right hand, and said *alvida* (farewell) to the old man. Fatima had her head covered with a greenish *dupatta*; one edge held by her teeth. It concealed her expression. There was no smile this time. She looked beautiful. Did I see a tear in her eye? I wasn't sure. I turned away, feeling somewhat sad at parting. Why would such a brief stay with this family affect me so deeply, I wondered? Perhaps it was the hospitality, care, and brief solace I'd enjoyed after a rough time. I turned south and began my gradual descent again, without looking back.

Rescue

I was quite exhausted from this weeklong ordeal. I had to find a way to surrender safely. The local military was rather trigger-happy for my liking. You couldn't blame them, though; they were on edge too, not knowing who would fire at them and from where. I had thought about it and decided to carry some white cloth with me. Fatima might save my life, perhaps. I continued walking, unsure of my direction, hoping desperately to meet some unarmed local administrative authority to surrender to. It was just a hope. And like all hopes, it was elusive.

About two hours into my descent, I noticed smoke and heard dogs howling and barking. It was possibly a village in distress. Fishing out my binoculars, I peered in the direction of the smoke. I could see the tops of houses from where I was. The smoke was coming from the houses, and nothing seemed amiss except for the frenzy of dogs. I walked for about ten minutes towards the smoke and began to see the village more clearly. I peered through my binoculars again and found the village to be devoid of any signs of human movement. Getting closer, I saw that the entire village had gathered in one open area. There were military guards encircling the crowd, and some military teams were moving tactically from one house to another, spending about ten to fifteen minutes in each dwelling. It was probably Shutmulla village, which the *Gujjar* family had mentioned. There was no way to be certain, though. I wondered what was going on— perhaps a search of the village houses, with the villagers out of the way. The area had seen a lot of action lately, courtesy of me; I smiled to myself. The military was probably searching for the other militants who had escaped from yesterday's firefight.

This might be my chance. I thought about drawing their attention with a few rounds of fire but dismissed the idea immediately, considering it too dangerous. They would love to bag another militant. I waited and watched, brainstorming ways to get their attention. I decided to move closer to the village. About half a mile away, I pulled out the white scarf Fatima had given me and began to wave it vigorously. I waved it for about five minutes intermittently, but nothing happened; no one noticed me. I walked closer to the village and repeated the exercise.

After a few attempts, someone in the crowd seemed to have noticed me. Suddenly, more faces turned towards me. I waved the scarf more vigorously. Now some guards noticed me as well. I could see one of the guards run to his superior, pointing in my direction. Thankfully, the distance between me and the guards was about six or seven hundred yards, with a steep gradient in between. I waved the white garment a few more times, wondering what my next action should be. From what I'd read in newspapers in Delhi, the military never spoke about captured militants. Only showed off dead ones, with arms and ammunition recovered from those killed, neatly arranged around them. I didn't want my weapons displayed alongside my body. I tore off a piece of the white scarf and hung it on a tree branch, I was taking cover behind. This was a clever way to ensure that they continued to see it. I also placed a half-filled magazine under the hanging white cloth. I was certain the military unit would view this suspiciously. The military patrols had been lured and ambushed many times.

I decided to climb back up to where I had first noticed the smoke this morning. Now began a long wait. From my position, I could not see any activity in the village area. I felt completely blind. I used this time to readjust the ammunition in my remaining magazines and to modify the load for easier transport should things go awry.

Late in the afternoon, I saw a cautious head peek out from the depression ahead. I pulled out my binoculars and gazed through them. I had to stifle a laugh. The fellow was ashen with fear, wiping the sweat from his brow with his sleeve even in this cold weather. He was looking around, utterly terrified; it almost seemed comical. This was a young lad who had been sent up first, and he didn't like it. Soon, I noticed another head emerge a few yards to the right of the first person. They were about fifty or sixty yards from the white cloth I had tied to the tree. They both froze. Soon, a third head popped up between the two. He was a bit further back. He pulled out binoculars and scanned the area. Then, he yelled some orders. This third guy was young—most likely an officer.

Soon, more scared-looking soldiers appeared. They were exercising extreme caution. Life is a gift and must be preserved for the sake of one's family for as long as possible. One of the men crawled toward the tree with the cloth on it. As he approached, he yelled something to his companions. I could make out the word "magazine" a few times. More military personnel had arrived in the area and took up firing positions. Soon, some soldiers began to spread out to their left and right, remaining under cover. By now, the place was teeming with soldiers. Some were more confident than others. Soon, the entire area was abuzz with military activity. The magazine had been picked up and was being examined. The white cloth had been removed, and three men were in an intense discussion, using the tree as cover. I decided to wave the remaining white scarf. It was immediately noticed, and everyone took some kind of firing position immediately. I yelled at the top of my voice in English that I was Ajay Rana, who had been kidnapped.

I repeated it again twice.

I heard a voice yell back in English, "Come out into the open with your hands up."

"I want to be sure you won't shoot," I answered in English.

"No, we won't," the guy shouted back in response.

"Please send an officer up the slope," I yelled.

"No," came the prompt answer.

"I'm surrendering my weapon and pulling back," I yelled.

"Okay," he said.

I left one rifle that I had not used, along with its magazine and an additional piece of white cloth draped over it for easy visibility. Then I withdrew about fifty yards. No sooner had I reached my new position than I saw the military arrive at the spot and take possession of the rifle. Having fulfilled my promise, I hoped they would trust me more.

"Send me an officer," I shouted again from my new position.

"Okay, I'm coming up," said a voice. "I'll bring one soldier along to cover me," he added.

I was in a good position to defend myself against the two, so I yelled back, "Okay!"

I saw two guys moving up towards me, each one taking position while the other moved. They approached about twenty yards from where I was. I asked them to stop. I could clearly see their bewildered expressions. The two also spotted me behind good cover, and they could see the weapon.

"Do you still have a rifle?" the officer asked loudly.

The loud volume wasn't meant for me but for his soldiers to hear that I was still armed. It was a precarious situation for them - they couldn't fire at me with two of their soldiers in between us. Any fire towards me could jeopardize their safety from either side.

"Yes, just to be safe and sure," I yelled back. "I am Ajay Raina," I repeated. "I want to be rescued," I said slowly, in a loud, clear, and emphatic voice.

This instilled some confidence in the young officer. He asked the soldier accompanying him to cover him and he rose from his position, walking confidently toward me. When he was about ten yards away, I too left my cover and stood up. He continued moving slowly towards me until we faced each other. I handed him my rifle, which he took and placed it on the ground. He then shifted his rifle from his right hand to his left and extended his right hand to me. We shook hands, both feeling relief from the immense stress and anxiety we had experienced over the past hour or so.

The officer then called out to the soldier accompanying him. The soldier got up from his defensive position and walked over to where we were. The officer asked the soldier to pick up the rifle lying on the ground and to assist me with all the items I was carrying. I handed over the entire load to him. With two rifles and my gear, the soldier was heavily burdened. The young officer gestured for us to walk down to where the rest of the team waited, tactically deployed. I followed him, and the soldier followed behind me. As we descended, the officer introduced himself as Captain Salil Gupta. Aside from that, no conversation took place. It was somewhat of a treacherous descent to where the rest of the force had taken up their tactical positions. It took us about fifteen minutes. Another officer greeted us while standing, while all the others crouched behind whatever natural cover they could find.

"Is everything okay, Salil?" asked the officer in Hindi.

"Yes, Sir," replied Salil. "Meet Mr. Ajay Raina," Salil introduced.

I extended my hand, and he shook it, introducing himself as Major Rajesh Thakur.

The soldiers seemed to relax a bit now. An elderly yet seemingly junior officer ordered someone to fetch some tea. He was a Junior Commissioned Officer, abbreviated as JCO. I knew that such officers rise from the ranks. They are very experienced and relied upon for it. Lukewarm tea from a thermos flask was served in stainless steel tumblers with sweet dough strips called s*hakarpara* in India. I now felt safe amongst these soldiers. I mentioned that I wanted to sit down. One of the soldiers grabbed a backpack and placed it for me to sit on. I thanked him. Major Thakur then asked me what I was doing here.

"I was kidnapped from a Sopore Hotel and have been on the run since," I replied in a mix of English and Hindi.

He wasn't surprised.

"Yes, we learned about all that from the local police and the Intelligence Bureau," he said.

At that moment, a soldier came up to Major Thakur, and I heard him say, "CO *sahib*," while handing him a wireless radio handset.

Major Thakur took the handset. They had a lengthy conversation about the situation. After their discussion, Major Thakur stated that we would have to wait here for a while. Their Commanding Officer (CO) was on his way and would soon be with us. Major Thakur gave some instructions to the JCO, who began to adjust and redeploy the troops.

In the distance, I could see a convoy of five vehicles approaching the village, with one fairly large van lagging behind. They neared the village and appeared to bypass it while heading toward our location. Major Thakur asked how I came to possess two AK rifles. I replied that I escaped with them. He looked puzzled, as did Captain Salil.

"I was held captive in a cave and chained," I explained. I then went on to recount my experience. "Did you find the two bodies in the cave?" I inquired.

Major Thakur turned a bit pale.

"We shot them" he lied.

"Yes, you did," I said. "Then there was that ambush you were in," I continued.

He listened without saying anything, quite puzzled and shocked that I knew about that as well.

"You were ambushed and pinned down," I said. "Then the militants ran away, leaving two bodies together. I was situated behind the militants and decided to help. You discovered the bodies later," I added.

Major Thakur and Captain Salil were silent. They exchanged glances.

"Go on," said Major Thakur.

"Nothing more. Now you have rescued me," I said.

He appeared slightly relieved.

At this point, the vehicles were once again out of sight, possibly obscured by the slope and the trees. The individual with the wireless radio informed the Major that the CO was enroute to the site. I was offered more tea, which I politely declined. A few minutes later, a group of soldiers arrived, followed by the CO and his entourage. There was a flurry of saluting and '*Jai Hind*' greetings, some acknowledged, and others ignored by the CO.

The CO looked at me but addressed the Major.

"Thakur, what is happening?" he asked in English.

Major Thakur gave the CO the gist of events while the CO kept scrutinizing me. After the Major finished explaining, he turned to me.

"Are you Ajay Raina from Nectar Juices?" the CO asked sternly.

"Yes," I replied firmly.

He then asked, "From Delhi?"

I responded, "Ji sir," meaning yes, sir.

He offered his hand, and I shook it.

"Colonel Sherawat," he introduced himself, gripping my hand firmly and shaking it vigorously. "Raina *sahib*, you are quite a brave person," he remarked.

It appeared that he was aware of what had happened. Maybe he had been updated via wireless radio or was aware of reality, as all COs usually are.

"Has Mr. Raina been given something to eat?" he asked, looking at Captain Salil, who scurried off to find food among the soldiers.

"Let's talk", said Col Sherawat.

Soon three folding stools were placed some distance away. The deployment of troops was readjusted.

"I'll get straight to the point," said the Colonel. "According to reports from the Delhi Police and the Intelligence Bureau, a terrorist named Ghulam Qadir Mir, code-named Musa, orchestrated your kidnapping in collusion with one Mr. Khan who is a senior person in your company. Terrorists and their Pakistani handlers use code names for their operatives on communication devices in an attempt to conceal their identities," he educated me. We monitor the conversation whenever we're within range and listen to what we can," the Colonel said. "The terrorists wanted the Jammu and Kashmir Police to release one Tariq Ahmed Lone, who was wanted for the killings of numerous policemen in Kashmir," he added.

The Colonel informed me that Musa has been quite active on the radio and other wireless equipment over the past week. For the first two or three days, he was negotiating with the police for my exchange.

Now, he was inquiring about my whereabouts from his supporters and the villagers after my escape. It was his radio communications and information from the Tangpora Police Post that led to the recovery of the two dead terrorists I had killed in the cave.

"We took credit for it," Colonel Sherawat stated.

"It's important that we appear to be dominating," he continued. "It's beneficial for you as well; it absolves you of any legal troubles," he added.

He also expressed his gratitude for my courageous action in rescuing his ambushed team.

"I hope you didn't lose any soldiers?" I inquired.

"No, thankfully we didn't. It wasn't a planned ambush by the terrorists; they just stumbled upon us, and an encounter ensued. They were on a convex slope and the fire was ineffective," he replied.

"The crux of the matter is that Musa is still looking for you, and we can exploit this to get him," he suggested.

"I have just been rescued," I protested.

At that moment, a flurry of activity occurred as two cylindrical boxes with peeling olive-green paint were brought to the site. It was late afternoon now. Some aluminium containers emerged from each box, which I realized were hot cases for food. Silence fell while two soldiers served us food. It consisted of *poories* (deep-fried flour pancakes, about six or seven inches in diameter) and some potato curry. I was quite hungry and quickly began to eat without waiting for others to be served. Any kind of food tasted delicious. After finishing the four *poories* I was initially served, I was offered more, but I declined. I drank some water and handed my plate to one of the soldiers, while others were still eating.

The Colonel also finished his meal and turned to me. "The guy who kidnapped you is still threatening us. We need to eliminate this threat," he said. You have done so much, so bravely, you can help us do this as well. "

I was quiet for a while and said that I wanted to go back to Delhi as soon as possible. My family must be so distressed.

"I can't stay here for days trying to help you eliminate an elusive Militant," I answered.

"Terrorist, not militant," he corrected. We refer to them as terrorists, he reminded me. "All I want is one day from you," the Colonel pleaded.

"What's the plan?" I asked.

"You," he said, "will expose yourself to the villagers. They will want to apprehend you and hand you over to Musa. You will then escape into the forest. Hopefully, Musa will come looking for you, since he desperately wants Tariq Ahmed released." Musa will be interested in capturing you alive to be of value. "It is then that we will ambush him," he explained.

"Am I to be a bait?" I asked.

The Colonel smiled and replied, "Yes, kind of."

"What if I say no?" I asked.

"Nothing, we go to the battalion HQ. I will inform my superiors and the police that we have rescued you accidentally. They'll debrief you, and you'll be on the next flight home. But Musa will be alive and planning another kidnapping. The new victim may not be as brave or as resilient and as ingenious as you, Raina *sahib*," he said.

This boosted my ego a lot.

"You are very convincing, Colonel *sahib*," I said, agreeing to the plan.

"We have no time to lose," he said to Major Thakur. "Where are your original clothes?" he asked me.

"With me," I replied.

"Put them on quickly," he said.

Bait

I walked up to the cloth bag I had been carrying and took out my soiled clothes. I went behind the largest tree and started to change. I felt both scared and excited at the same time. Colonel Sherawat was issuing hasty instructions to Captain Salil and Major Thakur. He asked us to pack up and be ready to move. I returned in my changed outfit and began to gather my belongings. A soldier approached me and said he would take care of it. I noticed admiration and respect in the eyes of the soldiers, who were now aware of everything I had endured and what I was capable of. I had the determination and courage that they look for in their officers. I was, in a way, a hero.

Soon, we were all ready to leave and began making our way down the hill to where the vehicles were parked. Just before we reached the vehicles, near the spot where I had initially drawn the attention of the villagers and the soldiers, a party consisting of Captain Salil, the JCO, five soldiers, and myself was instructed to halt. The others continued to their vehicles. Meanwhile, the force near the village, having either completed their search or abandoned it, was also loading up and boarding their vehicles. Shortly thereafter, the CO and his party zipped past the village. The other vehicles in the village also departed, taking the same route as the CO, and soon disappeared from sight. This created the impression among the villagers that the entire military force had left the area.

Captain Salil and I, along with his small party of six, were left behind. The sun was about to set. Captain Salil pointed to an isolated house on the outskirts of the village, about three hundred yards away, and asked me to go there and ask for food and to enquire about the nearest police piquet. He said he would send one of the soldiers with me for approximately fifty yards for my safety.

"He will cover you," he said.

I felt nervous again. Defenseless and naked without a weapon, I walked toward the house, feigning a limp. An old man was smoking a *hookah*, and some women were busy with household chores. As I approached them boldly, everyone stopped and stared at me. The old man yelled at me, demanding to know who I was and what I was doing in the village. I stepped closer and introduced myself as Ajay Raina, a Kashmiri from Delhi. I explained that I had been kidnapped by militants and needed food, as well as directions to the police piquet if there was one in the village. The old man and the women looked shocked. One of them began to speak hurriedly, urging the old man to get rid of me. She called out loudly to someone. Soon, a young man in his twenties emerged from a nearby field. The women told him something about a stranger pandit having escaped from the militants. He ran into the village, perhaps to gather more men to nab me. One of the women yelled at me to run away if I wanted to live. The older woman slapped her. I decided to run for my life. I had stirred up a hornet's nest as planned. I didn't want to take any more risks in trying to convince them further. I turned and dashed back into the forest. I reached the spot where the soldier accompanying me was waiting, and we both covered the three hundred yards or so to where Captain Salil and others were waiting. We were breathless. While I was catching my breath, Salil gave me his binoculars. I saw a mob with sticks, axes, and other tools gathering near the house where I was seen. They were excited and chattering away, spreading out in search of me. They approached the area where my companion soldier was covering me before we ran back. The sun was setting, and realizing it was a wild goose chase, they abandoned their search and returned to the village. Some remained persistent and continued to look for me.

At the village, there was a festive atmosphere. Through the binoculars, I saw someone with a walkie-talkie talking amongst the crowd and making some transmissions. I handed back the binoculars to Salil, pointing to the guy with a walkie talkie. Salil looked through the binoculars in the direction and confirmed that someone was indeed talking on a walkie-talkie. Captain Salil asked his men to move further up. I followed Salil. After about twenty minutes' climb, we saw a faint foot track and stopped. Salil went into a huddle with the JCO. They were perhaps discussing how to lay a good ambush here. After they had discussed the tactical matter, we moved about thirty yards from the track. Here we established a rest area. No one was allowed to even smoke here. Two soldiers spread out ground sheets for Captain Salil and me and provided us with two blankets. We sat down, and although I wished for a cup of tea or coffee, such luxury wasn't available here. I told Salil that I was mentally and physically exhausted and wanted to sleep. He handed me his backpack to use as a pillow. I lay down, adjusting the backpack as best I could, and pulled the blanket over me. I heard the *Azaan* in the distance, which was the last thing I heard before falling asleep.

I woke up in the night to see that everyone was turned in except for two soldiers who were awake and on sentry duty.

"What time is it?" I whispered to one of them.

He looked at his watch and said, "Four."

I got up and walked a few yards away to ease myself. When I returned, I found Salil peering at me. I went off to snooze again, and I guess he did the same. I heard the *Azaan* again, and I sat up. Everyone was up and packed except for me. I got up too. None of us had removed our shoes during the night. One of the soldiers passed around a stainless-steel plate filled with *shakarparas*, the sweet fried dough strips. Everyone had some, washing them down with water from their bottles. I didn't have any, so Salil poured some into a tumbler from his water bottle for me. The sun was rising now, and one could hear the roosters from the village. Except for the smoke, there was little activity.

Salil ordered us all to move to the track site. He laid the ambush tactically. One party of five was covering the track from about fifty or sixty yards, depending on the available cover. The JCO, along with another soldier, was deployed about fifty yards down the track in a similar manner. This smaller party was not meant to engage the targets, except when they were escaping from the ambush site. I still had to play the role of bait. The sun was up.

There was a flurry of activity in the village. Soon, men began gathering near the house from which I had run away. The youngsters were all excited; it was going to be a hunt of sorts. A lone vehicle was approaching the village now. It soon reached the village, and two armed men got out. The gathered villagers rushed towards them with cheers. Salil, who was watching all this through his binoculars, said that a discussion was taking place between the armed men and some village elders. Soon, the armed men began walking towards the house where I had gone for help. The two armed men were seen talking to the old man and the women. The old man pointed towards the track. The two armed men, along with about ten others, started to climb into the forest. The village crowd tried to follow them. One of the armed men turned around and shouted at them to go back. They all began to move back into the village but lingered in the distance. The two armed-men and their team started to climb again, widely spread out. A limping coward could not have gone very far, they may have thought. Every fifty yards or so, one of them would shout, "Oey Raina." They would stop and listen for a reply, but receiving none, they would resume advancing. When they were about a hundred yards from the ambush site, I called out.

"What is it that you want?"

Over the last few days, I had learned to manage my fear quite well, but my heart was pounding again. Was it fear, anticipation, or excitement? I couldn't tell. Perhaps it was a blend of all three.

"Listen, we want to talk to you," one of them said.

Maybe it was Musa. I had no idea.

"Why?" I yelled back.

"It isn't you we're after," he lied, climbing hastily now.

"You are armed and have so many people with you," I yelled back.

He and his team stopped for a moment. He signalled to the men accompanying him to return. They didn't turn back, but did not advance any further. The two armed men no longer needed a search party as they had homed in on me.

"We want you to help us get one of our companions released," he said. "You are also a Kashmiri and must help us. We won't cause you any harm. You are of immense value to us unharmed," he said.

All this time, he kept climbing along the path while I moved back up. I chose not to respond to him for a while.

"Oey Raina! Are you there?" he yelled again.

I had crossed the ambush line by about fifty yards by now.

"Yes, I am still here," I replied in a loud and clear voice feigning fear.

My fear had vanished after I had crossed the ambush line. I was now as excited as a hunter on a hunt.

"Listen, just wait where you are," he yelled.

"Okay," I replied.

From in between the trees and bushes, I could make out that their pace had increased. The village team was over a hundred yards away from the two armed-men pursuing me. My heart was pounding hard against my chest now. The duo was in the middle of the ambush site. Suddenly the sound of automatic fire disrupted the peace and quiet. The fire was unrelenting, some accurate, some not. The duo did not get a chance to even cock their rifles. They fell and wriggled about as bullets kept entering their bodies. The fire lasted for about a minute.

Salil shouted "Stop fire!" and the firing stopped, one odd round still being fired, perhaps accidentally.

I looked at the village search team. They were in full flight. It was hilarious to see them run. Some could have broken the Olympic record in sprinting today. I glanced further down to where the rest of the villagers had gathered for the hunt. They were also running helter-skelter back into the village. An eerie silence hung in the air. I got up and began to walk towards the slumped terrorists. Captain Salil asked me to stop.

"They may activate grenades", he yelled.

I couldn't give a damn now. Unarmed, I walked over to where they lay motionless, Salil shouting at me all the while to stop. I reached one of the terrorists and noticed my watch.

"He's wearing my watch," I yelled back to Salil.

So, this was Khalid, as I had named him. Known to the world as Ghulam Qadir Mir and to the Military as Musa. I turned him over with my foot and noticed he was still alive, breathing heavily.

I said in Kashmiri, "Can I have my watch back?" He blinked; his mouth wide open.

"I am here," I said, enjoying the moment.

He blinked again for the last time.

Soon, Salil joined me, followed by the others. Salil asked one of the soldiers to remove the watch from Musa's hand. He did so and handed it to me. I wiped it on my shirt and put it on. Everyone gathered, and the sloganeering and cheering began.

"*Bharat Mata ki Jai*!", "*Har Har Mahadev*!".

The soldiers were elated. Soon, the JCO, Shamsher Singh *sahib*, as Captain Salil referred to him, and his companion soldier joined them. However, Salil quickly got busy deploying the troops again to prepare for any surprise attack by the terrorists. It was time to break the radio silence they had observed so far, Salil made some radio calls. He seemed buoyed, and he lit a cigarette.

"You smoke?" I asked Salil.

"I don't usually," he replied.

I asked for one as well and enjoyed it after many years. I noticed some soldiers smoking as well. It had been a hard night and a very tense morning.

Salil asked three soldiers to head to the village to arrange for two cots. They left immediately. Not worried about revealing their locations, some soldiers lit a fire and began brewing tea. Salil and I sat down on the ground sheets.

"So, is this your first independent operation?" I asked.

He responded with an affirmative nod. He was happy, and it showed. It felt strange that we had killed two human beings yet were in such a joyous mood. It was the joy of knowing that it was them and not us who were dead. A solemn silence fell over us. Soon, tea was served, and it was very refreshing. The sweet *shakarparas* seemed to have run out. After about half an hour, we saw the three soldiers returning with two cots and eight villagers carrying them. It took another fifteen minutes or so for them to reach the site. The villagers carrying the cots seemed glum and scared. Around this time, a military convoy was spotted approaching the village. One of the soldiers pointed out the convoy to Captain Salil, saying, "CO *sahib*." The convoy continued past the village to the base of the forested mountain. The bodies were placed on the cots, and the villagers lifted them onto their shoulders, as the entire team began to descend towards where the vehicles had stopped. The movement appeared tactical, with the leading pair stopping and progressing one by one, covering each other.

As soon as we reached the base where the vehicles were parked, slogans and cheers filled the air. Chants of '*Bharat Mata ki Jai*' and '*Har Har Mahadev*' were shouted repeatedly by the frenzied soldiers. Colonel Sherawat first hugged me, then Captain Salil Gupta. Their battalion had made six kills in a week, which was a tremendous success for any battalion.

The bodies were photographed and loaded onto a military truck. Captain Salil explained that these would be handed over to the police for the postmortem and other civil administrative formalities. A short distance away, another military truck was dispensing breakfast to Captain Salil's team. They offered breakfast to the eight villagers who had helped bring the bodies down, but they declined the offer. Salil's team was being appreciated by just about everyone. A table and four camping chairs were set up. Breakfast consisting of scrambled eggs prepared with onions and green chilies, along with deep-fried multilayered flatbread called *paranthas*, was served. Hot tea was offered in porcelain cups. Colonel Sherawat invited me to take a seat first; he sat down next, followed by Major Thakur and Captain Salil. In a more peaceful time, this could have been a lovely picnic. I savoured whatever little I could eat. After finishing my tea, I requested another cup. Soon, everyone was preparing to leave. The chairs and tables were folded up and loaded back onto the truck. Colonel Sherawat asked his driver to sit in the cabin of the Suzuki Gypsy and took the wheel himself. He gestured for me to join him in the front passenger seat. An armed vehicle with a machine gun mounted on it led the way. Ours was the next vehicle, followed by another similarly armed vehicle. It appeared that the rest of the convoy was to follow separately. Major Thakur and Captain Salil were perhaps accompanying the rest of the convoy.

As we passed through the village, we could see silent, sullen villagers glaring at us. Col Sherawat opened the conversation, asking about my family, my job, and the purpose of my visit to the troubled state. In between my brief responses, he talked about his family and his unit, the 77 Rashtriya Rifles, the 77th Battalion of National Rifles, one of the many units specially created to combat insurgency and terrorism with troops drawn from the regular Army.

"The menace of terrorism has been created by the arch enemy Pakistan to bleed India," he said. "The cause espoused is religious separatism," he informed me.

I knew all about it, being a Kashmiri myself, but I played along.

I glanced at my watch. We had travelled for an hour and a half. A well-guarded military compound came into view. The gate swung open, revealing armed sentries. As we entered, there was a flurry of salutes and loud "*Jai Hind*" greetings. We stepped off in front of well-manicured flower beds. I followed the Colonel to his office. He removed his headgear and invited me to sit. Before sitting himself, he rang a bell from somewhere. A smartly uniformed soldier appeared, looking serious and anxious. The Colonel asked him to order some tea.

Colonel Sherawat sat down on his large office chair.

"Let's get to the point," he said. "Soon the police and perhaps the Intelligence Bureau guys will be here. Then there is a requirement to lodge a 'First Information Report' (FIR) with the police since it is a case of abduction," he continued. "So, what's 'our' story?" he asked.

While travelling I had some time to think things through. I knew he was worried about the four 'kills' his men had claimed. The battalion must have reported these to the higher headquarters. It would be embarrassing for the battalion if a controversy erupted, and doubts arose. It was in my interest to stay clear of the legal complications from the state police.

"Colonel *sahib*," I said, "I will keep the story simple. I was kidnapped from my hotel. I was blindfolded and taken to some remote location. I requested my captors to allow me to relieve myself. I escaped from there and continued walking and resting. A *Gujjar* family provided me with some food and milk on the second day of my escape, until I came upon this village. I tried to get help and some food, but the villagers' hostile behaviour made me withdraw back into the forest. I hid there until the next morning, when I noticed villagers and two armed men searching for me in the forest area. I climbed higher and chanced upon a military patrol. They provided me protection and searched the area where the villagers were hunting for me. After a while, I heard gunfire and was escorted down from the forest. I am extremely thankful to the military for rescuing me."

Colonel Sherawat rubbed his hands.

"Perfect," he said.

At this point, the tea arrived and was served with great care, accompanied by exquisite cookies.

"Ajay, we have a guest room prepared for you. We've also arranged a change of clothes. Please freshen up and join us for a late lunch," Colonel Sherawat said. "We anticipate the police and the IB officials will arrive late in the evening," he informed.

"Can I have my lunch in the guest room?" I asked.

"Of course," he replied.

He called someone, and an officer arrived. He escorted me to a well-appointed but simple guest room. A soldier was waiting there. He was to help me if I needed any assistance. Was he a guard? I wondered. I requested to be left alone and headed straight for the washroom. I brushed my teeth, shaved, and took a warm shower. After stepping out of the shower, I wrapped myself in a towel. I opened the wardrobe to find two sets of undergarments, a shirt, a pair of trousers, two pairs of socks, and a pair of handkerchiefs. There was a new leather belt as well. On one side of the wardrobe, a gown was hanging. I smiled at the impeccable planning and care from the Military. I put on the gown and waited for lunch. I heard a knock, and soon a person dressed in white set out my meal on the small dinette. The lunch was simple: lentils, mixed vegetables, yogurt, salad, and a few *chapatis* (a finer version of *roti*). I relished the meal. The individual in white returned to clear the table. I needed to rest, so I lay down on the bed, still in my gown. I think I fell asleep almost immediately.

I woke up to the sound of a knock. I glanced at my watch and saw it was a quarter past five. I opened the door. I was asked to come to the Commanding Officer's Office at six. Shortly afterwards, another guy appeared and handed me a cup of tea.

I dressed in the new outfit that had been set aside for me and headed out. I needed to orient myself. The guard directed me to the Commanding Officer's Office. As I entered, I noticed Colonel Sherawat and three others seated across the table. An empty chair was positioned for me on the side, allowing me to address both Colonel Sherawat and the people seated opposite the table. As I entered, all three stood up, and we were introduced. Mr. Munawar Mir served as the Superintendent of Police for the district, commonly referred to as the 'SP'. The other was Mr. Mathur from the IB, and the third was Mr. Abdul Bhatt, the Station House Officer, or SHO for short. He is the Police Officer in charge of the local Police Station and is considered the most powerful Government official in his beat after the SP. The SP began by apologizing for my kidnapping. He congratulated both Colonel Sherawat and me for the successful rescue operation.

At this, I noticed the Colonel shifted uncomfortably in his large chair. Mr. Mir, the SP, asked me to recount the entire episode, which I did, sharing the same narrative that the Colonel and I had discussed. Mr. Mathur then inquired about who had booked the hotel and arranged for the taxi. I explained that I had booked the hotel, but the taxi was organized by the hotel at the request of someone in our office. The information about the hotel booking is shared with the office of the VP, Administration for reimbursement of the amount owed to the hotel.

"I was, however, surprised by the initiative taken by someone to ask the hotel to arrange a taxi for me," I said.

Mr. Mathur asked me if anything seemed suspicious to me.

I responded, "Not then, but now the entire trip is suspicious. My captors knew my flight, my hotel, even my name."

"Do you know the purpose of your kidnapping?" asked Mr. Mathur.

"They wanted some Tariq released in exchange," I replied. "I heard this being mentioned by Ghulam Qadir outside the cave area when they were contemplating whether to kill me or not," I added.

The SHO had been taking notes on a pad all this while. Colonel Sherawat interrupted at this point and suggested that all of this be reported in the FIR at the local police station. He seemed eager to get rid of the police as soon as possible.

The SHO interjected and stated there was no need for a new FIR since one had already been lodged at the Sopore Police Station by the hotel manager immediately after the abduction. He recommended that I should provide a statement to the Sopore Police Station as an extension of the FIR. He appeared keen for the case to be handled by the Sopore Police. The SP nodded in approval.

"What are your plans for returning after you record your statement to the Sopore police?" the SP asked.

I replied, "I haven't had the time to think about it, but my safe return is my prime concern now."

He offered to provide me with security until I left the state. Lacking confidence in the local police, I looked pleadingly at Colonel Sherawat. He immediately understood my predicament and interjected, stating that security would not be an issue. He would arrange to escort me to Sopore to collect my belongings from the hotel, and for recording my statement at the police station and finally, to the airport. Perhaps Colonel Sherawat too wanted me to have minimal exposure to the state police. An awkward silence followed. The three stood up to leave, and Colonel Sherawat joined them. We all shook hands. Mr. Mathur mentioned that I would be contacted by some IB agents in Delhi in a few days. I nodded. Once they were gone, Colonel Sherawat sat down again and invited me to do the same. He inquired if I was comfortable.

"Yes," I replied.

I thanked him for his considerate gesture in providing clean clothes. I mentioned that my own old clothes had to be discarded as they were too filthy, and I would need to use the new ones until I retrieved my belongings from the hotel.

He said, "You are welcome. These clothing items have been specially purchased for you. They are yours."

"We are having a small party at the Officers' Mess tonight. The officers have invited you. It will be chilly in the evening. I will send you one of my pullovers," he said, inviting me. "Return the pullover when you leave," he laughed. "We are getting together at eight," he added.

I looked at my watch; it was already six-forty. I then asked him if I could speak to my wife from a telephone booth nearby.

"Certainly," he answered enthusiastically. "We should have thought about it earlier," he said.

He handed me a paper pad and a pen and asked me to write down my number. I did, and then I pushed the pad back. He called what I assume was his battalion exchange. He then asked me if I wanted some tea. I declined.

"I was served tea in the room before I joined you," I said.

While we waited for the call, he said, "The battalion is in an upbeat mood, because of you."

He admired the way I had escaped a near-death situation and acted so tenaciously over the week.

"You would have made a great soldier," he said.

There was no mention of the four terrorists I had killed, though. The telephone rang, and Colonel Sherawat handed me the handset. The operator asked me to wait until he connected me. Colonel Sherawat got up and left the office, keeping a gentle hand on my shoulder before leaving.

"Sir, go ahead," said the operator. By this time, Priya was frantically repeating, "Hello?"

"It's me, Priya," I said.

I did not get a chance to speak for nearly a minute as a barrage of questions came my way—some admonishing me, some asking if I was well, asking me to swear on God that I was fine. My truthfulness was also being questioned. I had to raise my voice somewhat to calm her down. I told her that I was well and safe.

"I will return by my scheduled flight tomorrow night," I said. "I can't tell you more since I'm not on a private line. Things have happened, and I'll tell you about them when I return."

"Mr. Khan told me that you had been kidnapped by someone, but he was not forthcoming about what they were doing about it," she complained. "It has been so traumatic for us," she said, sobbing.

I reiterated that I was fine and safe. I informed her that I was putting the phone down.

"Okay," she sighed.

I placed the phone in its cradle and stepped out of the office. Colonel Sherawat was speaking with Salil, who was a short distance away. He waved at me, and I waved back before making my way to my room.

While I waited in my room, a pullover was handed to me by the helper guard. I put it on and sat down to watch some TV before heading to the Officers' Mess. There was no mention of my abduction or rescue for the entire time I watched the news. I was indeed 'too small a person to matter,' as Gulam Qadir had judged. I switched off the TV and made my way to the Officer's mess, which was part of the same building complex.

The atmosphere at the party was jovial. Colonel Sherawat welcomed me in and announced my name in a loud voice. There were a lot of handshakes and introductions that I couldn't register so quickly. Some officers were in civil *mufti* and others wore uniforms; it was an operational area after all. Soon, an officer asked me what drink I would prefer. I inquired if the mess had 'Old Monk' rum?

"Of course," he confirmed. "It is our favourite drink here."

Old Monk rum has a loyal following in India. It's inexpensive, has a distinct aroma, and a mildly sweet taste. It was our favourite drink back in our college days too. In the corporate world, one must pretend to be sophisticated, and whiskey was the drink of choice there. I requested rum and club soda. A waiter dressed in all white served me the drink.

It tasted as good as it had in my college days. My spirits rose with each sip.

Everyone who met me praised my courage and tenacity, and what I had accomplished. No one mentioned the four terrorists I had killed, but they all knew about it. The awe in which they held me was quite evident. It seemed they considered me a gallant soldier, just like themselves. My self-esteem was at an all-time high, and the rum was certainly helping.

"What Battalion title should we give him, boys?" asked Colonel Sherawat.

There was silence, and then a young officer from the crowd yelled, "Deadly!"

"Deadly!" everyone shouted.

I had been renamed 'Deadly Ajay.' My feats of the past few days had been acknowledged.

Soon, dinner was laid out, featuring quite an elaborate menu. I was offered the first plate at the buffet and then guided to a seat at the dining table. I sat next to Colonel Sherawat, who was at the head of the table. The dinner was relatively quiet, with a laugh or two here and there. Colonel Sherawat informed me that Salil had been sanctioned thirty days of leave starting the day after tomorrow. He will escort me to the Sopore Hotel to collect my things and then to the Police Station to record my statement. After that, he will drop me at the airport.

"Isn't he flying too?" I asked.

He replied, "We don't get paid that well." "Salil will report to the transit camp in Srinagar after dropping you. He will reach Jammu by an escorted military coach and then take a train to his hometown," the Colonel informed me. After dessert, we all got up. "Coffee?" asked Colonel Sherawat.

"No, thank you," I replied. We shook hands, and I returned to my room. 'Deadly' Ajay slept very well that night.

The next morning, after a leisurely breakfast in my room, I walked out to where Captain Salil was waiting with two escort vehicles and one passenger vehicle. Colonel Sherawat and Major Thakur emerged from the Officers' Mess, came over and we shook hands.

"All the best," said the Colonel, giving my shoulder a pat.

I thanked him. We departed the complex in a convoy of three vehicles. I glanced at my watch; it was half past eight. I was seated in the rear seat to keep my visibility low, while Captain Salil sat in front beside the driver.

We arrived at my hotel around half past nine. As I walked in, there was a commotion at the reception. The manager was called, and tea was ordered. He was very apologetic, thanking Allah for my safety.

While we had tea, my baggage was brought out and placed next to the reception desk.

"Do you want to check your stuff?" the manager asked.

"There's no need," I replied.

I then thanked the manager for the taxi he had arranged to the airport and asked if there was any fare to be paid. He seemed surprised and said he hadn't ordered any taxi. He said that he was under the impression that I had hired the taxi myself at the airport. I thanked the manager for reporting the incident and lodging the FIR with local police.

"I informed your office as well," he said.

I thanked him again.

We left the hotel room and made our way to the police station. It seemed that the police station had been informed to expect us by the superintendent's office. It took about an hour to record my statement, which was done in Urdu script. I signed it and requested a carbon copy, which was signed by the officer in charge of the police station and handed to me. I folded the papers and placed them in my briefcase.

We now headed to the airport. The two-hour drive was scenic and pleasant as we passed through the outskirts of Srinagar. Salil and I exchanged our opinions about the heavenly place Kashmir, which had, unfortunately, lost its tourist value due to the militancy sponsored by Pakistan.

Having dropped me off at the airport, Captain Salil left. I checked in and got busy with the security clearance. Once I reached my departure gate, I decided to call Priya from the airport public call booth. She picked up the phone and began to admonish me once again for not calling sooner. When her anger subsided, I reassured her that all was well and that I was at the departure gate awaiting my flight, which was likely to depart in another hour and a half. She told me not to hire a taxi.

"We're coming to pick you up. Mr. Khan will be taking us to the airport," she said.

I fell silent for a moment. "Fine," I replied.

I sat down in the waiting area and started thinking about the last few days—they had been traumatic, hectic, uncertain, and life-changing. What was now bothering me was who ordered the taxi. I tried to connect the dots. It became clear that it was a set-up—but by whom and why? 'Why,' I knew. I was abducted to free Tariq. By whom? It needed to be confirmed.

When boarding was announced, I returned to the present and chose to enjoy my flight home. I set aside all thoughts of the events of the last few days. During the journey back, I celebrated my freedom and my life.

Back Home

After landing, I collected my baggage and walked out to see Priya, Rohan, and Rhea waiting in the reception area. I hugged Rohan and Rhea. Priya had tears in her eyes as she smiled at me. Rohan took charge of my suitcase. Mr. Khan offered me his hand, and I shook it. We all began to walk towards the car park in a rather awkward silence, which was finally broken by Mr. Khan.

"Thank God you are safe. We were so shocked to hear what had happened to you," he said, interrupting the silence. "Even more shocking was the demand," he mumbled.

I gestured for him to stop, and he complied. The ride home was a quiet affair. Rohan was inquisitive. I briefly explained that I had been abducted immediately upon arriving at the hotel. Perhaps my abductors did not want to lose me if I started to move about looking for suitable land. They wanted to grab me as soon as I arrived. I wonder who informed them. I shared this with Rohan so that Mr. Khan could hear it too, sparing me from having to repeat myself later.

"They wanted some Tariq chap to be released from prison," I told Rohan.

"Yes, I received the call and informed Farookh *sahib* immediately," Mr. Khan interjected.

Mr. Farookh Ahmed Mattoo was the Chairman and Managing Director of 'Nectar Juices' Private Ltd. Our company had three juice extraction and packaging plants.

Our juices were sold in Tetra Packs of various sizes. Our product was nationally renowned and trusted by consumers. It was a family-owned business. Mr. Farookh Ahmed Mattoo, affectionately known as Farookh Shaib or Mr. Farookh by most, was of Kashmiri descent but seemed to have little to no interest in Kashmir, as far as I knew. I was tasked with selecting the land for the fourth plant in Kashmir.

"Farookh *sahib* informed the Police Commissioner about the abduction without delay," said Mr. Khan. "He even attended a meeting with the Police Commissioner and IB officials the next morning to organize your rescue," Mr. Khan added.

I kept listening and absorbing all I could. Near our home, I asked Mr. Khan if we could discuss it in detail the next day. Rohan protested; he wanted to hear everything now.

"I'll tell you all about it at home," I assured Rohan.

Over a wonderful dinner, I spoke about my ordeal, my escape and rescue by the military. It was the same story I had told the police. My children and Priya listened with rapt attention, their faces occasionally turning pale. If things had gone differently, Priya would have been a widow today, struggling to provide for my children.

I enjoyed a leisurely bath and retired for the day in the arms of the one I loved most. I began to sob in her bosom. I had been through a lot and much had changed within me. She cajoled me calmly like a mother would. I drifted into sleep in my familiar bed after ten days of a harrowing experience.

Answers

After a wonderful morning tea with family and feeling very thankful to be alive and with them, I dressed and had breakfast. I was ready to leave for my office, not so much for work but to seek some answers.

Our offices occupied the top two floors of a five-storied building that the company had leased for thirty years. The fifth floor had a staircase leading up to the roof, which some staff used to take cigarette breaks away from disapproving eyes. The building had a two-level parking lot in the basement. The ground floor housed various shops and showrooms, while the upper floors were occupied by commercial offices of several small turnover companies.

Our Managing Director, Mr. Farookh Ahmed Mattoo, occupied the top floor along with his personal staff, as well as the Chief Financial Officer Mr. Ravi Dubey, HR Head Arun Rastogi, and their teams.

This floor also featured the conference room and a small tearoom for senior executives. Mr. Khan had an office here as well. All other employees were situated on the fourth floor in cramped cabins or partitioned offices, which also included a cafeteria with a self-serve tea and coffee machine and a seldom-used water cooler. On the ground floor, there was a popular coffee shop called "Coffee Break', where employees from across the building enjoyed their breaks and casual dates with colleagues. It was a lively, classy, and tidy spot. An old rickety elevator with sliding grill doors, operated by an attendant, served our two floors - primarily intended for individuals with offices on the fifth floor. Everyone else was expected to use the stairs – a tedious climb for the more heavily built among us, but it did help keep us fit.

Mr. Yunus Khan enjoyed the designation of Vice President (Administration). He was the man Friday to the MD, Mr. Farookh. Everyone who was subordinate to him addressed him as Mr. Khan, if not Sir. The other two Presidents were for Marketing and Operations and were usually out to visit the plants or marketing zones.

My job was to assist Mr. Khan with administrative tasks. It involved the administration of the local office and some aspects of the administration of the three plants. I also took care of some personal matters of Mr. Khan and Mr. Farookh. The plants, two in Himachal Pradesh and one in the Meghalaya state of India, were quite autonomous and had their own Plant General Managers (GMs) and dedicated administrative and HR Staff. Mr. Khan reported directly to Mr. Farookh.

I arrived at the office a bit late. I had been a victim of an abduction while on the job and was trying to leverage that situation. The entire staff on the floor shook my hand and expressed concern. They all wanted to know what had happened. So, word had spread.

I shook some hands and acknowledged others with my eyes and eyebrows. Then, in a loud voice, I announced "It was nothing. Three people tried to abduct me, and they took me somewhere. I managed to escape and eventually encountered a military patrol after a few days of wandering, who then rescued me. Here I am, back without completing my assigned job. I still have no answers to many questions myself just yet. So, let's get back to work".

Having put this behind me, I went to my desk and pretended to focus on my work. An office boy approached me and informed me that Farookh *sahib* would like to see me. I went to the fifth floor and knocked on Mr. Farookh's office door. He invited me in. Mr. Khan was seated across from him. As I entered, Mr. Farookh stood up and extended his hand to me, expressing his happiness at seeing me safe and unharmed. I shook his hand, thanking him for his concern. He gestured to a chair next to Mr. Khan, and I pulled the chair and sat down.

"I was so shocked and concerned when I heard about your abduction from Yunus. I immediately called the Police Commissioner and reported the matter to him," he said. "The Commissioner held a meeting with the IB and me the following day. By then, he had sought and received information from Sopore. The Police Station had reported to him that a 'First Information Report' (FIR) had indeed been lodged by the local hotel manager regarding my abduction by the militants. The IB officer advised us to remain calm and not to overreact. He expected the militants to renew their demand soon through another channel," Mr. Farookh narrated.

According to Mr. Farookh, he received another call from the abductors that evening and informed the caller that he was in contact with the authorities to secure Tariq's release. However, this process would take some time.

"Thereafter, there were no calls, and I was very worried," said Mr. Farookh.

Mr. Khan then interjected and said they would have tried everything to get me home safely, but I was not convinced.

"Who ordered the taxi for me at the airport?" I asked, surprising both.

They were shocked at the question and looked at each other.

After a momentary delay, Mr. Khan said, "Perhaps the hotel did."

I let the question be. I generally knew what had happened, but I needed a few days to comprehend things in detail.

Mr. Farookh mentioned that I could take a few days off if I wished. I declined.

"I truly apologize again for what you went through," he said, indicating that the meeting was over.

I stood up and returned to my desk. Just then, my phone rang, and the exchange operator said that one, Mr. Sarin wanted to speak with me. I asked him to put me through.

"Hello, is this Mr. Raina?" the caller on the other end inquired.

"Yes," I replied.

"I'm Resham Sarin," he added.

"Yes, Mr. Sarin," I responded.

"You know Mr. Mathur in Kashmir; he advised me to contact you about the land you were interested in buying in Sopore. I do not want your bids at this moment. Do you understand? We can discuss this over lunch at 'The Bites' restaurant near your office at one o'clock today. Don't reply now, just come," he instructed, hanging up without giving me a chance to respond.

It felt like it was a coded message, and the caller perhaps didn't want the operator to understand it. I was certain this was a call from the IB. It meant that investigations were underway, and I might soon receive some answers from a premier national intelligence agency.

At half past twelve, I informed a colleague sitting closest to me that I would be out for about two hours. I requested that he not disclose this information until someone asked. I made it appear that I was bunking the Office. I knew no one would contest my absence or other discretions for a few days. After all, I had been through a lot for the company.

I reached 'The Bites' restaurant in time. A well-dressed tall gentleman waved to me from a table deep inside the restaurant. I walked up to him and asked, "Mr. Sarin, I presume"?

"Yes", he answered. "That was for anyone listening in on that phone line. I am Resham Khanna," he said.

After we shook hands, he gestured for me to sit down and asked what I would have.

"I'll have a chicken sandwich and coffee," I answered.

Excellent choice," he said.

"Do you want me to answer some more questions?" I asked him, point blank.

He smiled and said, "Maybe one."

The waiter arrived, and we fell silent. He placed two glasses of water on the table and waited for us to order.

"Two grilled chicken sandwiches and two cappuccinos, please," said Khanna.

"The question is, who ordered the taxi to pick you up?" Khanna asked.

I said I didn't know. I had asked Khan this question, but he seemed unaware. In my opinion, no one could have ordered the taxi because it required his clearance first.

"That's the key," Khanna stated. "Now let me share what we know," he continued.

"We know that someone orchestrated this kidnapping or abduction, however you prefer to label it. We are also aware of the reasons behind it. It was a conspiracy, a very serious crime. We need to identify exactly who or who all did this," he said. "It's a matter of national security and we will need your help with this," he said.

The waiter arrived with our sandwiches, prompting us to pause our conversation. He then shared that they, in the IB, were suspicious of my version of my escape. The villagers of Tangpora had notified the police about the gunfire they heard, and the police subsequently requested the military to come and investigate. My expression must have changed because he smiled mildly. I was astonished by the information he possessed and his analysis of the facts.

"We won't take away the military's credit," he continued, "nor will we charge you with murder. After all, it was done in self-defence. But murder it was."

It was a sugar-coated threat. I listened in silence as he waved his hand towards the sandwich while taking the first bite. Our coffee arrived, giving me time to think. I detested being blackmailed. I was starting to feel anger build within me. He must have noticed a change in my expression again; he looked at me and changed the topic, complimenting the sandwich. I decided to bat on the front foot.

"Do you have witnesses to corroborate 'your' theory of my escape?" I asked, confronting him.

This time, it was his turn to be surprised. The blood seemed to drain from his face as it turned ashen. He appeared visibly uncomfortable being challenged. Regaining his composure quickly, he stated that the objective was to identify who all were behind this ghastly attempt at my life and eliminate the threat. I remained silent.

"Try to identify the person who informed the militants of your arrival at the hotel. This guy will lead us to others involved," Khanna said. "The Kashmir IB and my office in Delhi will conduct our own investigations. Keep your eyes peeled in the office for more information," he advised. "We are in the process of checking the calls made from your company and from the homes of the suspected employees."

I remained silent and simply nodded in agreement.

"Your MD is of Kashmiri descent, although he has been living in Delhi since birth," he said, indicating that Farookh was an obvious suspect. "Yunus Khan also needs to be watched," he added.

He then paid the bill in cash. He handed me his card.

"Feel free to contact me," he said.

We shook hands, and I walked out.

When I returned to the office, my colleague informed me that Mr. Khan had come looking for me. I called Mr. Khan on the internal network.

"Sir, were you looking for me?"

"Yes," came the reply. "Mr. Farookh is inviting us to dinner tomorrow at his place. I wanted to pass along his invitation to you," he said.

I was thrilled to hear this. I had never been to Mr. Farookh's home. Receiving an invitation to his home was a rare honour.

That evening we went out for dinner. I forbade the family from discussing the events of the past few days. These events were behind us, and we were together—that is what mattered. It was truly wonderful to be with my family. I looked at my two children and wondered what would have befallen them had something happened to me. My lovely Priya would have been burdened with caring for my children while needing to work to make ends meet. She could have been exploited by her employers. My children might, perhaps, have quit their studies midway. Anger began to swell within me at whoever was responsible for having offered me as bait to some terrorist without thinking of the misery it would cause my family.

"Is anything wrong?" asked Priya, perhaps sensing my anger.

"No, it's nothing," I lied. I was just thinking that I need to increase my insurance,"

I told the children that Priya and I were invited to dinner at Mr. Farookh's residence. The children initially protested but soon began to chuckle together at the prospect of an unsupervised evening they would enjoy at home.

That night, I went to bed with two decisions to work on: to enhance my family's financial stability at any cost and to seek out and confront the entities who were prepared to sacrifice me for whatever reason.

The next morning was normal, it was a quiet day at the office. I tried to catch up with my work. I left the office earlier than the others since I was to dress appropriately, with a fresh shave and all, for dinner at Mr. Farrokh's. Priya, too, was expected to fuss over her outfit and take time dressing.

After dressing, we took turns looking at the mirrors. Finally, we left for Mr. Farookh's house at about seven p.m., leaving an adequate margin for the notorious Delhi traffic.

Mr. Farookh's house was an elegant bungalow in the Diplomatic Enclave, a highly prestigious area in New Delhi. He inherited a portion of it after his father's demise. His father was a prominent mid-level politician and industrialist. He lived on the ground floor, while his younger brother Omar occupied the first floor. The property featured manicured lawns and gardens, along with a row of staff quarters at the back for their numerous servants.

We parked our car on the premises under the guidance of a security guard. A liveried attendant opened the door for us. As we walked in, we were greeted by Mrs. Mattoo, a very elegant lady, perhaps in her late thirties or early forties. Dressed in a light pink chiffon sari adorned with floral patterns, she appeared more stunning than any model I had ever seen. Her long neckline was adorned with a string of pearls. The bun at the nape of her neck looked exquisite. Her figure could serve as a benchmark for judging beauty queens.

With wide, welcoming eyes, she approached Priya and embraced her, both exchanging compliments. I think Priya noticed that I was somewhat awestruck by Mrs. Mattoo's beauty, as I caught a playful smile on her face. Mrs. Mattoo then turned to me and said, "Hello, Ajay."

"Hello, Mrs. Mattoo," I replied.

"Call me Mehtab," she said, extending her manicured, soft hand.

I took her hand in a gentle grip before letting go. Her handshake felt firmer than mine and more welcoming.

"Oh, please sit down," she said. "Farookh *sahib* has just come home. He is freshening up, and it shouldn't be long before he joins us," she added.

The drawing room was elegant as well, radiating old-school charm with large Persian carpets. An elegant chandelier hung in the centre. The hall featured two seating areas, and we were being hosted in the larger one.

"So," she turned to me, "I believe you had quite a harrowing experience during your visit to Kashmir. I've been told you were almost abducted," she remarked in a mildly concerned tone.

So, the whole episode was gradually being diluted, I thought. "Yes," I replied briefly.

The door was opened again by one of the servants, and Mr. and Mrs. Khan appeared. Mehtab got up to receive them as well. She walked up to the Khans and greeted them just as she had greeted us.

"Hi Shyama, you're looking wonderful," she said, holding her. "It's been a while now. Where have you been hiding?" she asked.

They seemed to be well acquainted and very friendly. Mrs. Khan was elegant too, her brown hair beautifully complementing her deep skin tone. I greeted her as well.

"Yunus tells me that he would be severely handicapped if you weren't around," she said.

"He is kind to me, Mrs. Khan," I replied.

"Call me Shyama," she said.

At this point, Mr. Farookh arrived, smiling and apologizing for being late.

"I have to do all the work at the office, you see," he said sarcastically—or so I hoped.

He asked each of us what we would like to drink. He was followed by a waiter who heard what we ordered. It was whiskey all around.

"It is wonderful to have you all over. This was much overdue," said Mr. Farookh.

Mehtab asked the ladies for their preferences and insisted that they all have wine. The drinks were served. Small talk followed about children, schooling, and how handful these kids could be.

"Why only kids? Even the menfolk are quite a trouble," said Shyama, looking sternly at Mr. Khan.

Everyone, including Mr. Khan, laughed.

"You've been through some adventure. We are glad you are okay," said Mrs. Farookh while trying to pay special attention to me.

I merely smiled. So, it was now being termed an adventure, I thought. What a systematic way to tone things down over scotch and snacks. The snacks were exquisite, and the sit-down dinner that followed was fabulous. It included Mughlai and Kashmiri delicacies. The crockery was fine China, and the cutlery was silver.

All of us left Mr. Farookh's house around eleven. On our way back, Priya mentioned how welcoming and great hosts Mehtab and Farookh were. She remarked on their affluence, which she credited to their wealthy ancestry.

"You seemed to be overawed by Mehtab's beauty," she said, looking at me accusingly.

I did not look back and pretended to keep my eyes on the road. After a pause, I dared to say that a beautiful woman is a beautiful woman.

The children were disappointed that we had returned home so early and that their unsupervised period had ended.

Investigations

The next morning, two sleuths led by Mr. Khanna arrived at the office. They met Mr. Farookh and requested to question me and Mr. Khan. Mr. Farookh had no choice but to consent. My questioning commenced first. It felt like a mere pretence since I had already given my statement. The only question they posed was whether I knew who had ordered the taxi.

"No one in the office knows," I replied. "Mr. Khan is the only one who could have been aware of my hotel and flight details and most likely ordered the taxi. I suppose he seems to have forgotten that he did."

Mr. Khanna then asked me to send Mr. Khan in, which I did.

Having left the makeshift interrogation room on the fifth floor, I returned to my table and tried to catch up on the pending work. After about an hour, I noticed the investigation team leaving. Soon, my phone rang. I picked it up; it was Mr. Khan on the other end.

"Come up to my office, will you?" he said.

"Yes, Sir," I replied.

I hung up the phone and went to his office on the fifth floor. A very shaken and distraught Mr. Khan sat behind his desk, his water glass nearly empty. He didn't offer me a chair.

"What did you tell them?" he asked in an agitated tone.

"Nothing except what happened," I answered.

"Why are they harping on who ordered the taxi?" He almost yelled. "I didn't, I swear, I didn't!"

I pulled up a chair and sat down.

"Sir, relax; they are doing their job," I said, trying to calm him down.

He rang the bell and asked the office boy to bring him some water and a cup of tea, his tone angry. I told Mr. Khan that I had nothing to do with this investigation. Even I was subjected to silly questions as if I had orchestrated my own kidnapping. This will go away soon, after they file their report. He seemed to calm down somewhat. I got up to leave. While leaving, I mentioned that someone who knew about my flight arrival may have ordered the taxi. Mr. Khan's face turned pale again. I was almost certain now that it was the terrorist organization that had ordered the taxi based on information about my flight and hotel. I did not go back to my table but headed to the 'Coffee Break' in the commercial area on the ground floor to grab some coffee and a sandwich for lunch.

During my lunch break, I tried to analyze Mr. Khan's behaviour. If he had nothing to do with my abduction, why was he so upset about the line of questioning from the IB and police investigating the matter? I thought the answer to my questions might lie with Mr. Khanna. The rest of the day passed without any significant events, and I returned home. I had a shower and enjoyed the evening with Priya and the kids.

If I weren't alive today, my family would be planning my prayer meeting. Every moment with my family now had a new meaning.

I decided to take the next day off. Mr. Khan gladly accepted my request. I fished out Mr. Khanna's visiting card, called him, and requested a meeting. He agreed and asked me to come to his office at eleven.

I informed Priya that I had taken a day off and was going to meet some people who wanted to offer me a new job. If anyone from the office asked, you could tell them that I have some banking matters to sort out. You do not know anything further. I left home with a swarm of questions swirling in my mind.

I arrived at Mr. Khanna's office around five minutes late. It was located in a poorly maintained, rundown government building. However, his office was tidy and well-organized. He welcomed me, and we shook hands.

"Care for some tea?" he asked me. I declined, explaining that I had just had my breakfast before leaving for his office.

"So, what can I do for you?" he asked.

I hesitated a bit and then said that I wanted answers.

"Answers to what?" he asked.

Without waiting for me to respond, he went on to tell me that it was a setup to get one Tariq released from prison.

"His full name is Tariq Ahmed Lone, code name 'Mustafa.' He is not a significant terrorist. About ten days before your abduction, the district police arrested Tariq with a pistol and a grenade, based on information provided by a family member to Mr. Munawar Mir, the SP. After your abduction, the hotel notified the local police and Mr. Munawar Mir about it. The terrorists' demand for Tariq's release was also communicated to the SP late that night through some informants. The reality is that both Tariq and you were minor players and did not warrant the urgency demonstrated in the abduction of more prominent individuals. Even your company did not create enough uproar to secure your release. My guess is that you were used as a feeble attempt to get Tariq freed. If it didn't work, you were to be killed, ensuring that the authorities take the next kidnapping for Tariq's release more seriously."

I listened with rapt attention. A chill ran down my spine after hearing his last sentence.

He then went on to tell me that they had records of several calls made by Mr. Khan to a few phones in the Sopore area a few days before I was sent there. Everything was coordinated through a local teacher named Ghulam Rasool.

"In a nutshell," he said, "you were not supposed to be back alive."

He said that he was certain that Khan was involved in my abduction and that Farookh might have sanctioned it. He said his department began a background check on Farookh immediately after my abduction and that they have clues that he has been sending funds to some charitable organization sympathetic to the separatist cause in Kashmir from time to time.

"Does all this answer some of your questions?" he asked.

I was silent for a long time.

"What can we do about it?" I inquired.

"Nothing," he replied. "The police could get Khan to talk after making an arrest, but no one will allow the arrest without sufficient proof. You are not an important person. You don't matter," he said, pointing his hand at me. "They played it well," he concluded.

He rang a bell and ordered tea without even bothering to ask me. He knew I would need it. Over tea, he asked me about my family. Just as I was about to finish my tea, he spoke again.

"Who fired a couple of bursts in the cave three days after your abduction?" he asked. "The villagers said they heard firing even before the Army arrived in the cave area."

I was stunned. This was the second time he had asked me about it, casting doubt on my escape story. He smiled knowingly.

I regained my composure and replied, "I don't know; I had escaped before that. Maybe the terrorists fought amongst themselves," I suggested.

"Possible," he agreed.

We shook hands, and I left.

On my way back, three things haunted me: first, I was not important enough; second, I could do nothing about it; and third, most scary, I was not supposed to have returned alive.

I *had* returned alive. Now I wanted to address the other two issues of being important and acting against the traitors. The children were at school. I opened a bottle of beer and invited Priya to join me. She declined the beer and made herself a lime and soda. We had a leisurely afternoon, and I decided to take a nap after lunch. By now, I had most of my answers and was starting to get an idea of what to do next. The children returned from school late in the afternoon, and we spent some quality time together that evening. I didn't believe much in God, but I was thankful to him nonetheless that I was safe and with my family.

Revenge

I lay down to sleep but could not manage to for many hours, consumed by thoughts of my helpless plight. I was being offered as bait to save someone who was prepared to kill innocent people. There was nothing I or the authorities could do. It was a bleak situation. When I finally slipped into sleep, disturbing dreams disrupted it. The three issues seemed to haunt me even in my dreams: 'you are not important enough,' 'you can't do anything about it,' and 'you weren't supposed to return alive.'

The next morning, while I was having tea, a vague plan began to form in my mind. I decided to call Mr. Khanna before leaving home for the office.

"Khanna *sahib*, it's me, Ajay," I said in response to his greeting.

"Yes, Ajay, go on," he replied.

"I'm sorry to call you so early. I couldn't have spoken freely from my office phone later," I explained.

"Go ahead," said Khanna.

"Please ask Mr. Khan to come to your office just once and ask him if he let my itinerary be known to someone intentionally or inadvertently," I requested.

"Why?" Khanna asked.

"I wanted you to observe and judge Khan's reaction," I said. "It might also put him under pressure, and he may reveal some aspects that we aren't aware of so far," I added.

There was some silence. "Okay," said Khanna, "just this one time." I thanked him and asked his permission to put the phone down. I hoped that Khan would reveal something or take some steps to help unravel the mystery.

Mr. Khan had a habit of going to the roof of the building two or three times a day for a smoke. He would sometimes call a staff member up there to discuss matters or give instructions. I thought he might call me up and disclose something to me in the privacy of the rooftop.

At around eleven, the office boy from the first floor informed me in a rather agitated and loud voice that Mr. Khan wanted to see me immediately.

"Why are you so loud and agitated?" I asked him, almost admonishing him for the way he conveyed the message.

"He is livid, and I, too, have been subjected to his wrath without reason," he replied.

I now knew that he had received Mr. Khanna's call. I was told that I would find Mr. Khan on the roof where he had gone for a smoke. I walked past the fifth-floor entrance to the roof and saw Mr. Khan sitting on the rear service lane parapet, smoking.

"What do the IB guys want from me?" he almost shouted at me. "Why do they think I am involved?" he asked.

I pretended I had not understood the context.

"What happened?" I asked.

He went on to tell me that he had just received a call from Mr. Khanna from the IB, who wanted him to visit his office this afternoon for more questioning. He further said that he was contemplating hiring a lawyer. I advised him to stay calm. I said that even the police and IB guys are under pressure and must show they have made enough effort before they close a case. Be calm and pleasant when you visit his office. Khan seemed to relax a bit.

"Thank you," he said abruptly, avoiding eye contact and indicating that I could leave.

I felt humiliated by this sudden dismissal.

Just as we were about to leave the office, Mr. Khan barged into my cabin and claimed in front of everyone that he had made a big mistake by sending me to Kashmir. He should have gone there himself. These stupid fellows think I sent you up there to be abducted. I can't bear these insinuations anymore. I don't know what to do. Everyone was standing in their cabins, aghast, having heard every word he uttered in anger.

"Did they confront you with the record of phone calls to Ghulam Rasool, the teacher?" I asked loudly for all to hear.

"What?" Mr. Khan replied, shocked and turning pale. "What calls?" he demanded, staring sternly at me.

I did not respond.

Realizing that everyone on the floor was overhearing the conversation, he walked out as quickly as he had entered. I was almost certain he was heading for the MD's office.

The following day, Mr. Khan arrived late at the office. Perhaps he had an early morning meeting with a lawyer. I went about my business until I received a call from Mr. Farookh asking me to come to his office. I immediately complied. The office boy opened the door for me, and I was asked to take a seat. He said he would get straight to the point.

"This incident of your abduction is disrupting the company's efficiency and causing rumours. Mr. Khan is also under pressure from the authorities, who have their own axe to grind," said Mr. Farookh.

He wanted me to downplay the entire issue.

"We can continue as usual and advance in our careers without disruptions," he stated.

I was being offered an olive branch alongside a threat.

"Yes, sir," I replied.

"Thank you," he said, indicating the end of the meeting. I got up and left.

As I was leaving the fifth floor, I noticed Mr. Khan heading up to the roof for his usual smoke. I hesitated and thought for a moment, then decided to go up to the roof as well. I saw Mr. Khan lighting a cigarette while sitting on the rear parapet as usual. He saw me and gestured for me to sit next to him.

I moved closer, bent a little as if to touch his feet, and then lifted both his legs over the parapet.

As Khan went down, I heard a weak scream followed by a thud. I immediately turned back, took the stairs, and went past the fifth-floor entrance, past the fourth floor, and down to 'Coffee Break' on the ground floor. I ordered a cappuccino and a sandwich. While my order was being prepared, I started to hear commotion outside. Such disturbances are commonplace in India, and no one pays much attention to them. I collected my order and walked to the elevator, asking the operator to take me up to the fourth floor. Since both my hands were full, he obliged. Upon reaching my cabin, I smiled awkwardly at the colleague next to mine and told him that I had received a dressing down from the top boss.

By now, there was some real commotion. Some people from the fifth floor were rushing down, while others on our floor were on their phones, then hanging up and hurrying down. One colleague mentioned that Mr. Khan had fallen off the roof.

"Suicide?" I asked loudly.

"Maybe," he replied.

Another colleague asked no one in particular, "Why did he do it?"

I had taken a big bite of my sandwich and was munching on it. The office was nearly empty by now. Leaving the rest of my sandwich on my table, I decided to go down and look, coffee still in my hand.

In the service lane behind the building, a crowd had gathered. Some were colleagues, while others were passersby. Mr. Khan lay in a pool of blood. No one dared to approach his lifeless body. Some were saying they had called for an ambulance and informed the police. Many of my colleagues saw me with coffee. I soon discarded my cup after a final swig, tossing it into a drain like most irresponsible Indians of the time did.

Mr. Farookh, along with security personnel, arrived at the scene. The HR fellow was frantically dialling someone. Many, including Mr. Farookh, looked up at the spot from where Mr. Khan might have jumped. Mr. Farookh was seen gesturing to one of the security guards to go up and check. About ten minutes later, a police van arrived, followed by two ambulances from different hospitals as a result of multiple calls. The area was cordoned off. Mr. Khan was placed on a stretcher and taken away in one of the ambulances. The outline from where Mr. Khan was lifted was marked with chalk by the police, and the area was segregated with tape. Soon, a convoy of police vans and two cars arrived, carrying senior police officers to the scene. The constables accompanying them asked us to disperse while they investigated. Soon, the crowd started to go back to their day, since there was nothing of interest left to see anymore.

I also returned to my desk and carefully placed the cash receipt and coffee bill into the drawer. Soon, a police constable came up to our floor and informed us that none of us were to leave without permission. He went to the fifth floor and notified them as well, or so I presumed. After a while, many policemen were heard climbing up to the fifth floor. The senior police officers must have come up on the elevator, of course. They were there to examine the spot from which Khan had jumped or fallen. I knew they would find numerous butts of Khan's brand of cigarette at the same location, making it easy to determine the exact place from where he may have leaped. There were murmurs and discussions on our office floor, and many eyes turned toward me as well. I decided to join in.

"Mr. Khan should not have felt responsible for my ordeal," I said to the colleague nearest to me. "The police doubt everyone."

I concluded by saying that he should not have taken such a drastic step. I remained silent thereafter and listened to others' conversations. I heard the same words and sentences I had used being repeated by others too. It seemed to be working, I thought.

Over the next four hours, many were questioned, and some statements were taken randomly. My statement was written down in greater detail, in which I described my ordeal in Kashmir and the questioning of Mr. Khan by the Police and the IB. When asked specifically where I was when the event occurred, I said that I was with Mr. Farookh. After that, I went down to the 'Coffee Break' to get some coffee and a sandwich, which I ate at my desk.

Finally, the employees were allowed to go home around ten at night. Mr. Farookh asked me to stay back. He called me over, and I met the local police officer leading the investigation. The police officer inquired if I had given my statement.

"Yes," I replied.

He mentioned that I might need to provide further clarification if required. I nodded and asked him if Mr. Resham Khanna from the Intelligence Bureau had been informed about Mr. Khan's death.

"He was also investigating him," I stated.

The inspector looked taken aback.

"You might want to discuss the case with him as well. He may have insights that could shed light on why Mr. Khan did what he did."

Regaining his composure, the police officer responded, "Fine, I will check with him too. Any information is welcome," he commented, smiling.

Mr. Farookh informed me that Mr. Khan had been declared dead by the hospital to which he had been evacuated. He mentioned that the postmortem would take place tonight or early next morning at the Civil Hospital. I was to collect the body from the hospital in the morning and take it to Mr. Khan's residence.

"Please assist the family in organizing the funeral. I am heading to his house now to break the news to Mrs. Khan," he said.

I had called Priya earlier in the evening to let her know I would be late. I rang her up again to say I was headed home. Priya had heard the news from other wives and confronted me with a barrage of questions. I told her I was very tired, both physically and emotionally. I had a whole lot to do the next day and asked her not to pester me for now. I suggested a quick dinner. I poured myself a whiskey and soda, took a big swig, and settled down on my favourite sofa.

I had managed it well so far.

I felt no remorse. I had indeed turned deadly.

By the time I had my second drink, a simple dinner had been served. I had my dinner, took a shower, and went off to sleep without waiting for Priya.

Priya and I both woke up early. I had to arrange a hearse and collect the body from the government mortuary after the postmortem. Priya decided to go to Mr. Khan's house to be with the grieving family. We had tea and light snacks and left home in two separate taxis. I didn't use my car since I would have to be with the body in the hearse when it came home. When I reached the mortuary, Mr. Khan's eldest son was already there.

"Hi Rafiq," I said when I saw him.

He ignored me. Rafiq Khan, about 23 years old, was a medical student at one of the prestigious local medical colleges. I went about the formalities to have the body released. The medical staff and police had us sign a bunch of documents. Soon, we had the body in the hearse. Rafiq and I were alone with the body in the vehicle, while others who had come to assist were leaving the mortuary in their own cars or two wheelers.

"I can't believe this has happened," I said, trying to initiate a conversation.

There was no response from Rafiq. I realized I had been painted as a villain by Mr. Khan to his family. He must have ranted about why I was casting aspersions on him while raking up the taxi issue and having the IB question him. Clearly, Khan was worried that his connections with the terrorists would eventually be exposed. I made no further attempts to engage Rafiq in conversation.

Many relatives helped us lower the body from the hearse and lay it on the *veranda* of a three-storied house built on a 200-square-yard plot worth many million rupees in this prestigious Delhi neighbourhood. Undoubtedly, he was a man worth far more than his salary would have allowed him to be.

The entire colony seemed to join the relatives in paying their respects and condolences to the family—so typical of India. Most colleagues were also present. I, too, approached Mrs. Khan to condole the death but was met with cold, ignoring looks. Soon, Mr. Farookh, accompanied by Mehtab, arrived. Mehtab and Shyama hugged each other, and Shyama broke into loud sobs.

In the afternoon, the *janaza* (funeral) procession left for the burial site next to a mosque. After lowering his body after religious rituals, all of us offered three hands full of earth into the grave after Rafiq and Taufiq, Khan's other sixteen-year-old son had done so. Soon, everyone began to disperse. I requested a lift from a relative back to Mr. Khan's house to pick up Priya and return home. On our way back in a taxi, Priya asked me if Mr. Khan and I enjoyed friendly relations. I told her that he was my boss.

"But why the cold shoulder for us?" she asked.

I had no answer to this heavily weighted question. I hoped no investigator would ask such a question.

"Maybe he was being questioned about my abduction by the police," I said after a pause. "Maybe he had something to hide," I added.

"Could that be such a strong reason to commit suicide?" she questioned.

"Depends on how deeply he was involved," I answered.

We were silent all the way home. Upon reaching home, the kids were curious. I had cautioned Priya to say the least and not to opine too much. I asked Priya if she could brew some tea and get me something to eat. It was my way of disrupting the children's curiosity and taking Priya's mind off the matter.

The next morning, I had my breakfast in a sombre mood and departed for the office. The atmosphere there was equally gloomy. We all got busy with our tasks. Around noon, I received a call from the HR head asking me to come up to the fifth floor. Mr. Farookh wanted to see me. I felt my heart sink and my morale take a hit, as if I were going to be fired or, worse, accused of murder.

I rose listlessly, almost dragging myself up, and climbed the two flights of stairs to the fifth floor. The HR head, Mr. Arun Rastogi, was waiting for me at Mr. Farookh's office door. I greeted him, and we both entered Mr. Farookh's office together. He gestured for us to sit down while he signed some documents. We waited until he finished. It was a long, agonizing wait full of uncertainty for me, during which I hid my nervousness as best as I could.

"Well," Mr. Farookh began. "The last few days have been particularly harrowing, and I anticipate this trend will persist for some time as the investigations continue. We must all take these disruptions in our stride, and the company must function as it did before," he said.

My apprehension eased slightly.

"We need to fill the void created by this accident," he said. "Khan relied heavily on you," he added while looking directly at me. "You were always aware of what he undertook as part of administration and other tasks," he stated, maintaining eye contact.

"Ajay, I am appointing you as the VP in place of Mr. Khan. In due time, you and Mr. Rastogi can select a suitable person to assist you. Your salary will be the same as Mr. Khan's," he mumbled. "Mr. Rastogi will issue the necessary orders regarding this. Please shift to this floor by the end of the week. Make sure to continue to look after the needs of Khan *sahib's* family," he said.

I was in shock. This was rather unexpected. I thanked Mr. Farookh, and he waved me away. It was time for us to leave his office.

I opened the door for Mr. Rastogi, and we both walked out. Rastogi turned to me and said, "Congratulations," in a rather sombre manner.

I thanked him in an equally sombre tone. I did not return to my office. Instead, I took the elevator, instructing the operator to take me to the ground floor. Upon leaving the elevator, I entered 'Coffee Break,' ordered a coffee, and sat down alone to reflect.

I was beginning to realize the importance of what had happened. I had removed someone who would have orphaned my children. I had taken his place. It was a sweet revenge, and I felt good. I was inching up the ladder, on my way to securing a better financial status, as I had promised myself for my family. I also felt a sense of relief. Expecting to be fired or worse, I received a promotion instead. It was an incredible feeling that couldn't be described in words but could only be felt. Still lost in thought, I was called to collect my coffee. It was time to go to my cabin. No one seemed to know what I knew. I went about my work normally. I also began to clean up my desk discreetly.

That evening, I went home via Mr. Khan's residence. The family was in mourning, and more relatives seemed to have arrived. I was met with hostile looks. I asked Rafiq if I could be of help. He asked me to order twenty simple meals for the relatives who had come. I was pleased to assist.

"Certainly," I replied.

I got into my car and drove to the nearest restaurant, where I ordered twenty respectable yet modest meals. I had the food packed along with some disposable plates and cutlery before heading back to Mr. Khan's house.

After delivering the food, I gave my card to Rafiq and said, "Please feel free to call me if you need anything."

He nodded in response. I was relieved that the hostility had somewhat subsided.

I arrived home late, and Priya was waiting anxiously. I told her why I was late. She, too, felt relieved that the Khans were reposing some faith in us now.

In the evening, I broke the news of my promotion to Priya. Given how it had come about, the poor thing could not enjoy the news. She was happy but could not express it. I said that we should keep the news from the kids until I shift to the fifth floor. She agreed. I was happy, and so was Priya. Celebrating happy couples usually have wonderful nights.

I visited Mr. Khan's residence before heading to the office. I was greeted more warmly than before. Rafiq requested my assistance in obtaining the death certificate from the hospital and the municipal authorities. I assured him that it would be taken care of. Upon reaching the office, I asked an employee to hire a taxi on company billing for the day, take Rafiq along, and collect the necessary documents. I also instructed him to make enough attested copies for Mr. Rastogi, the bank, and the family to address the legal issues regarding his will, among other matters. This employee I had selected was familiar with navigating government offices and the way matters were handled in India, including the use of bribes. He seemed a bit surprised by my authoritative tone. It was coming to me naturally.

Investigations Again

Just before our lunch break, the police arrived again. The inspector in charge of a local police station, along with a sub-inspector, a head constable, and two men in civilian clothes, were present. The inspector informed us that the individuals in civilian clothes were forensic experts. As the head of administration, I offered to show them around. We went up to the parapet on the roof and pointed out the location where Mr. Khan used to smoke; the cigarette butts were still there. I indicated the chalk body marking on the road below, which had begun to fade. One of the men in civilian clothes thanked me and said they would take it from there. It was a sign for me to leave, as they likely wanted to recreate the scene and sequence of events privately. Before leaving the site, I asked if I could order some lunch for them, but they declined. The senior police officer and the others continued their investigation and left the premises after about two hours.

The office memorandum regarding my promotion to VP of Administration was issued late in the afternoon. There were some half-hearted congratulations here and there, but the news was not received as well as it would have been in a happier situation.

The next day, as I was packing up from my fourth-floor desk to move to the fifth-floor cabin, I was interrupted by a call asking me to come upstairs. The Deputy Commissioner of Police (DCP), along with the officer in charge of the local police station, were once again waiting for me in Mr.

Farookh's office. My heart sank again. The forensic team had been here yesterday. They might have made some discoveries. Had Mr. Khanna given them some adverse input? As fear gripped me, my mouth went dry. I hoped my happiness over the promotion wasn't short-lived.

When I entered Mr. Farookh's office, the uniformed police officers were finishing their tea. They had likely been there for some time, I guessed. What had they discussed, I wondered. I greeted everyone and was asked to take a seat. The DCP got straight to the point.

"Mr. Raina, where were you when this incident happened?"

I tried hard not to swallow and betray the anxiety I was feeling. I think I succeeded in maintaining a straight face.

"I was at my desk having coffee and a sandwich when we heard the news," I said.

"You got these from the 'Coffee Break' shop on the ground floor, I suppose?" he questioned.

I answered in the affirmative.

"Did someone see you there?" he asked.

"Yes, the person at the cash counter," I replied. "My purchase and time would be on their record. And I used the elevator to come up. The operator was there," I added.

"Am I a suspect here?" I asked.

"No, not really, just ruling out some possibilities," the DCP clarified.

"Where were you before you went to the coffee shop?" the other policeman asked.

"I was with the MD discussing some matters," I answered.

"Do you remember what those matters were?" he asked.

I pretended to think.

After a brief pause, I replied, "Efficiency in the office."

"Yes, we were discussing ways to improve efficiency in our various offices and plants," Mr. Farookh interjected.

My alibi seemed to be holding, I thought.

"We've had a meeting with Mr. Khanna of the IB as well, and we are aware of certain facts that we would prefer not to disclose or discuss since they pertain to national security," the DCP added.

Hearing this, Mr. Farookh's face went pale for a moment.

"Well, there are three possibilities. The first is that someone went to the roof with Mr. Khan and pushed him over. The second is that he was disturbed due to an investigation by the IB, as suggested by his behaviour on the day of his death according to various staff members in their statements, and may have committed suicide, or that he fell accidentally," the DCP opined. "If someone pushed him over the parapet, we must know who that person was and what the motive was," he added.

My heart began to sink again, and my lips dried up for the second time. There was an awkward silence now. The officer in charge of the local police station broke the silence.

"Sir," he addressed the DCP, "we don't have any motive here. Things clearly point to the last two possibilities. It does not matter what we assume here. In both these scenarios, the case will be closed. Why tarnish Mr. Khan's reputation and jeopardize the insurance claim by the Khan family?" he summarized.

The DCP thought for a while.

"Well, then it's an accident," said the senior police officer with finality.

I noticed that Mr. Farookh was looking thankfully at the officer in charge of the police station, who gave him a subtle smile. The heavy bribe that must have been given to him had paid off. I hoped the investigations were finally over and the case was now closed. There were some handshakes. I offered to escort them out. I guided them to where the lift was and joined them in it.

"Ground floor," I instructed the operator.

Upon reaching the ground floor, I accompanied them to the waiting cars. The drivers were waiting for their officers with the car doors open. I escorted the DCP to his car with a blue pennant. He turned around once more for a final handshake.

"You are a very brave man, Mr. Raina," he said, smiling.

I did not know how to interpret that statement. The officer in charge of the police station saluted the DCP and walked to his vehicle a few feet away, just waving at me as he got in. Both were gone. I heaved a sigh of relief. I decided to visit 'Coffee Break' again for some quiet time.

That evening, the office boy helped me move to the fifth floor, which had been cleared of Mr. Khan's stuff. I sat down in the chair and felt uncomfortable. I decided to order a new chair tomorrow. After all, I was the administrative head and enjoyed considerable discretionary powers.

Priya and I debated whether we should go out to celebrate or not. We decided against it. We explained our sentiments to Rohan and Rhea, promising a lavish dinner when I got paid as VP next month. They understood.

The next few days were spent organizing myself in my new position. My interactions with Mr. Farookh increased considerably. I knew that, in due course, he would want to get rid of me. He suspected that I knew too much about his connection to the Kashmir Militancy. He may have also feared my interactions with the IB. He needed to find a suitable person to replace me, but until then, he wanted to utilize my experience in the company to fill the void created by Mr. Khan's death. He was forced to play along and humour me. I estimated that it would be a year before he could create a situation to replace me. I decided to deny him that opportunity.

On a Monday, a week later, I received a call from Mr. Khanna.

His first words were, "Well played, Ajay," followed by a knowing laugh.

A chill ran down my spine. What was it now? I thought. "Khanna *sahib*, happy to hear your voice." I lied, regaining my composure.

"Are you really?" he asked, laughing.

I was nonplussed. Before I could answer, he told me that the teacher, Ghulam Rasool, had spilled the beans regarding my kidnapping case. He said that our initial apprehensions were correct: I had been sent to Kashmir as a pawn to be abducted for Tariq's release. I had known this firsthand all along.

"Oh! So that was correct," I replied.

"There's another piece of news," Khanna continued. "Tariq has escaped," he said, laughing again.

What was there to laugh about concerning a terrorist escaping? I thought.

"Oh?" I answered.

"He will be neutralized tonight," he added.

I remained silent. The intelligence agencies often resort to such methods. They will squeeze the information from a militant or terrorist and announce to the world that he has escaped, only to eliminate him a day or two later to avoid difficult questions in court or to the media.

"I thought I would update you," he said.

I thanked him. He inquired about the well-being of my family, and we exchanged some small talk before ending our conversation and hanging up. I felt mentally drained after this call. What did Mr. Khanna mean by 'well played'? Did he know what I had done? Or was it just a guess? Then the reality began to dawn on me. He was aware of my actions in Kashmir through Mr. Mathur of the IB. He knew what I had done and what I was capable of. He had made an accurate guess about what might have happened. I also realized that there was nothing he could do about it. I felt better at that thought.

I now began planning my long-term survival in the company until I had an alternative livelihood. I thought of using the information I had from Mr. Khanna. Could I blackmail Mr. Farookh into permanently retaining me? I will have to plan it so that it does not appear to be so.

After our lunch break, Mr. Farookh's office boy came up and said that Farookh *sahib* wanted to see me. I immediately went to his office. He asked me to sit down. He began giving instructions to acquire some additional hardware for our Meghalaya plant, near Shillong, and to hire some software experts to assist with the installation. He further said that a similar upgrade was needed for our Himachal plants as well.

"Consult the plant GMs for their requirements," said Mr. Farookh. "Make sure they don't go overboard," he concluded.

Mr. Farookh expected me to leave, but I took a while getting up.

"Anything else?" he asked.

"Sir, I thought I should inform you that the teacher, one Ghulam Rasool, who was involved in passing information about my arrival to the terrorists has been arrested," I replied.

The colour drained from Mr. Farookh's face for a moment, but he regained his composure almost immediately. "How do you know?" he asked. I said that Mr. Khanna informed me. "Oh!" he responded. I then got up and left the office.

I was able to convey that the investigations into my abduction were still underway, that the middleman may squeak, and that I could not, therefore, be dispensed with just yet. He needed me to remain abreast of things and ensure that I did not place the blame on him.

I attended to some professional work and went home soon after Mr. Farookh left. Over tea, I asked Priya if we should consider moving to a better neighbourhood and a larger apartment. The children were growing up and needed their privacy. So far, Rohan and Rhea had been sharing a room in our three-bedroom apartment because we wanted to use one of the bedrooms for our frequent guests. Relatives from all over India visiting Delhi preferred to stay with us rather than in hotels. Priya was instantly excited about the prospect.

"Can we afford a bigger apartment?" she asked.

"Yes, the house rent allowance (HRA) on top of the salary is much higher in my new position," I answered. "Start looking," I added. "This will be your assignment," I said, laughing.

She replied with a hearty "yes," as enthusiastic as a teenager.

The only thing bothering me now was the reason why Khanna kept me in the loop of the investigation. The only answer that sprang to my mind was that the IB was keeping an eye on Mr. Farookh, and they might require me at some stage. If that was the case, it suited me just fine, so I dismissed the IB from my mind. I decided to cross these bridges when I came to them. After a refreshing shower, I sat down on the balcony to enjoy my whiskey. Priya and the children joined me, carrying their own drinks and snacks. I was so glad to be alive, surrounded by the family I loved dearly.

The next morning, I went to the office via Mrs. Khan's place. She welcomed me and asked if I would like some tea or coffee. I declined.

"I've just came to check on you. I've had my breakfast," I told her.

I asked her if there was anything she needed or if anything needed to be done. She fell silent. After an awkward pause, she mentioned that while the insurance amount she had received was substantial, it wouldn't last long. There were recurring needs of growing up children in the crucial stages of their education. I nodded in agreement.

"Should I raise this issue with Farookh *sahib*?" she asked. "It would be very awkward for me to do so," she added. "I never imagined that Yunus would leave us," she sobbed.

"I will see what I can do, Mrs. Khan," I said.

"Call me Shyama, please. You are like a brother. Can I call you *Bhai sahib*?" she asked.

I smiled and replied, "Yes, of course, Shyama. But I think I will leave now."

"*Khuda Hafiz*," she said.

She smiled as I walked to my car. While driving, I wondered about the change in her demeanour. What could have prompted such a shift? Perhaps she was aware of her husband's leanings and was attempting to salvage the situation as best she could for the sake of her children. Maybe they now understood that my abduction was instigated by him. Perhaps they wished for me to sympathize with the family and not rake up past events to protect the careers of her two sons. The reason could be any one or all of these. It didn't matter to me; I held no malice towards the family at all.

After about two hours at work, where I focused on the administrative aspects of the three plants, I decided to meet Mr. Farookh. I called him and asked if I could come by. He told to come in about half an hour, as he was about to have phone conversations with his Plant GMs. After about forty minutes, I asked his office boy to announce my arrival, which he did. I entered the office, and Mr. Farookh, still on the phone, waved toward a chair asking me to sit.

He hung up and said, "Yes, you wanted to see me."

I hesitated briefly.

"You're building up suspense," he remarked with a smile.

"Sir, I visited Mrs. Khan on my way to the office to check on her," I informed him.

"That was very good of you," he responded appreciatively.

I explained to Mr. Farookh that while the Khans were financially comfortable for now, the loss of regular income will dilute their savings in due course. With two children at the crucial stage of education, it would become challenging for Mrs. Khan to manage without exhausting her savings.

"What do you suggest?" Mr. Farookh asked, in his usual direct manner.

"Sir, we run three creches at our three plants. Although these are routinely inspected at the local administrative level, it would be beneficial to have someone visit these periodically, not just to inspect but also to identify ways in which we could improve them," I suggested. "We could appoint Mrs. Khan as a welfare officer who could visit our plants and interact with staff to see how we could assist them further. This would provide Mrs. Khan with a change from her routine and mundane life and a salary. A trip once a quarter should suffice. She could come to this office to submit her reports and suggestions at her convenience," I added.

Mr. Farookh looked at me for a moment and said, "Brilliant idea! What grade should we assign her?" he asked.

"Assistant manager?" I replied, framing it as a question rather than a suggestion.

"She was a VP's wife; we can't do that," he cautioned.

"She hardly has any work," I countered.

"All right, I'll discuss it with Rastogi and his HR team," he said.

"One more thing, Sir, it would be a lovely gesture if you and Mrs. Mattoo could visit Mrs. Khan and deliver this good news to her yourself," I suggested.

"Brilliant again," he responded.

I left feeling satisfied that I was able to address Shyama's request so promptly.

Feeling satisfied with myself, I decided to visit 'Coffee Break' and took the elevator down. On my way back up, I stopped on the fourth floor to say hello to the colleagues with whom I had worked shoulder to shoulder for years. While working on this floor, I often thought about improving this cafeteria. I decided to raise the issue with Mr. Farookh regarding new dispensing machines that would offer multiple options for both hot and cold beverages. I knew he would approve the welfare measure without hesitation. After spending some lighter moments on the fourth floor, I went up to my office and began thinking about the larger apartment we wanted to move into. Though I had asked Priya to select one, I couldn't help but browse some sites myself.

My phone rang, and the operator informed me of a long-distance call for me, then patched me through to the caller. It was Mr. Mathur of the IB Sopore.

"Yes," I replied.

"Hello Raina *sahib*, I am Mathur. How are you?"

I became apprehensive.

"Hello Mathur *sahib*, how are you?" I answered, pretending enthusiasm.

"I wanted to give you some news," he said.

"Go ahead," I replied.

"Tariq, that Tariq Ahmed Lone, for whose release you had been abducted, had escaped custody. He was spotted in a forest near the prison and has been neutralized" (which meant killed), he gloated. "I thought you would want to know," he added.

I fell silent for a moment and said, "Thank you. It's not a matter for me to rejoice over, Mr. Mathur, but thanks nevertheless," I blurted out.

"I can understand. It's quite traumatic," he remarked before ending the call.

So, my guess was right. The escape and all that was for public consumption. The fact that the IB was keeping me informed bothered me considerably. I began to feel that uncanny sensation again, that they were planning to use me as an asset or bait, and I didn't like that notion one bit. An asset meant a guy who could be used for their dirty work. There was no way they could blackmail me into doing anything, and I resolved to resist if it came to that.

An Informer

After a few weeks, while Priya was busy looking for a bigger apartment, I settled into my new role at the company and got on with the job effectively. Priya had nearly completed the selection of an apartment in a prestigious housing complex in South Delhi. It was a spacious four-bedroom apartment on the third floor, featuring a balcony that offered a view of the treetops outside. This space provided privacy and a sense of living in harmony with nature. Each bedroom included an attached bath, and we were in the final stages of negotiating the rent along with other terms and conditions.

We moved into our new rented accommodation by the end of June. The monsoons were around the corner, and the Koel birds announced it. Priya was renovating the interiors with new curtains, upgraded furniture, and electronic kitchenware. The kids were calling their friends over to show off. Life had taken a turn for the better. I was glad to be alive and with my family.

On Saturday, 24th June, at around 9 PM, I received a call from Mr. Khanna requesting a meeting the next day. I asked him what it was regarding. He replied that it was nothing serious yet, but it might become one soon.

"Khanna *sahib*, I want to live in peace and be left alone," I pleaded.

"That is fine, Ajay. It is up to you. You are a brave and fortunate person to be alive today despite a deadly conspiracy hatched against you. Many innocent people are not so fortunate," he said.

"What time and where?" I asked curtly.

"My office at eleven," he replied in equally curt tones.

"I'll be there," I said.

"Thank you, Ajay," he said and hung up.

I had a restless night. Even Priya noticed and asked if I was feeling well. I finally decided to dismiss all thoughts. I would eventually get all my answers, and I was finally able to sleep in the later part of the night.

I got up later than usual. I told Priya that I had a supplier to meet and would be leaving by ten. Could she whip up some breakfast for me despite it being a Sunday, a brunch day for the family? After breakfast, I set out for Khanna's office. The government office complex was nearly empty, with offices locked. Khanna's office was open. He greeted me, and we shook hands. He began exchanging pleasantries, but I cut him short and asked him why he wanted to see me. He pulled out a file and said,

"Your boss has been sending cash to some unknown entities in Kashmir. We have evidence that this is being routed to militants," he added. "Details are all there," he said, pushing the file toward me.

I opened the file and saw rows and columns filled with dates and figures. It appeared that cash was sent every quarter. The amount remained the same each time: five hundred thousand rupees, almost ten thousand US dollars, a substantial amount of money at the time. After I closed the file, Khanna handed me another one. It contained only six entries and seemed to show cash received by Mr. Farookh through couriers that had been sent to Kashmir. This amount was significant, ranging from ten thousand dollars to fifteen thousand dollars.

"Why should I believe you?" I asked, closing the file.

"Open the second file again," he said.

I complied. He pushed a piece of paper and a pen toward me and said, "Please note down the dates." I hesitated. "Go ahead," he urged. "Check the record of Khan's absence from the office, either on leave or on tour, when you go to your office tomorrow," he asserted.

I was now almost convinced of the authenticity of the IB investigation, so I noted the dates.

He then went on to tell me that they got onto the case after my abduction. Mathur suspected that it was a setup, which it turned out to be. He gave this input to us, and the IB began probing Nectar Juices, Farookh Mattoo, and Yunus Khan. A serious and confidential dialogue with the CFO Mr. Ravi Dubey followed, and everything came tumbling out. "It's not without reason that your company is making good profits while no other company in the same industry is doing as well," he said.

There was a long and awkward silence after he was done speaking.

"I'm sorry I can't offer you a cup of tea because it's Sunday. You know how the government offices are," he said apologetically.

"It's all right," I replied.

I got up, we shook hands, and I walked out of his office feeling quite pensive.

I reached home and opened myself a beer to cheer my mood up. Priya and the kids were doing their own things in the privacy of their own rooms, oblivious to the world outside. The privilege of a big apartment. I rummaged through the kitchen for leftovers from brunch with moderate success. I sat down on the balcony to enjoy the beer and watch the birds go about their business. I was now eager to find out about the dates Khanna had asked me to note down. Things were serious but interesting.

It was normal for Mr. Khan to visit plants and meet with the fruit vendors who supplied our plants with seasonal fruit in bulk. However, having exact dates on which the money was moved was crucial for IB. I could check the dates, but I had no way of knowing whether the money was received or sent. I approached the accounts branch employee working under the CFO, Mr. Ravi Dubey, and asked him for details of the expenses Mr. Khan had claimed for his travels over the past year. I explained that I needed this information to plan my future travel budget. After about two hours, I received an

Excel sheet over the LAN network that provided details of date-wise travel claims made and the destinations. The list contained about twenty-two entries from the last twelve months, and the dates of six of those entries matched the dates given to me by the IB. I decided to have a conversation with Mr. Dubey.

I walked into his office and said, "Sir, I thought I would have a cup of tea with you and ask if there is anything I could do for your branch."

He welcomed me, and we shook hands. He rang a bell for the office boy and ordered tea and cookies.

"Very thoughtful of you, Ajay. Everything is fine. I won't be here for long. You could ask the new CFO what he wants done for the accounts branch and our other staff," he said somewhat dejectedly. "Don't tell the boss yet, but I am planning to resign as soon as I have something lined up," he confided.

"Why?" I asked.

"I'm sorry, but I can't disclose the reasons," he replied.

The tea arrived, and he remarked that it was very brave of me to have escaped from the clutches of the militants.

"It must have been harrowing," he said. "You must tell us about the entire incident in detail over drinks or something," he requested.

"Sir, I saved my life, roamed around for a week, and was nearly killed again by the villagers and later by the military," and I don't know who was behind it," I continued.

Mr. Dubey's was sullen. "I wish I could explain," he blurted out in anguish.

The rest of the teatime was spent skirting the topic. We sipped our tea while engaging in small talk. Finally, I stood up to leave.

"Look for another job, Ajay," he suddenly advised.

This was the moment.

"Mr. Dubey, please resign if you find a better job, but don't resign out of compulsion," I said emphatically. "We must be seen to be on the right side. That is the only way to rectify the wrongs done in the past," I added before walking out.

His expression was one of utter shock.

Just before closing time, Mr. Dubey walked into my cabin and said we should talk alone somewhere.

"Any time," I answered.

"I'll let you know," he replied and left.

The week passed by uneventfully.

On Saturday, Mr. Dubey called me on the internal office line to invite me to lunch on Sunday at the Chelmsford Club.

"Be there at twelve," he said. I thanked him.

The Chelmsford Club is a classy colonial establishment with a dress code and rules. I arrived at the club at twelve. Ravi Dubey was waiting for me in the lounge. We shook hands, and he guided me to the bar. While he opted for a gin and tonic, I chose my preferred Golden Eagle beer. It was time to say cheers. We then found a quiet spot in the corner and sat down. The waiter brought the menu, and Mr. Dubey ordered some French fries and a platter of kababs.

"So," he began after taking a sip of his drink, "I feel very vulnerable working with the company," he sighed. "I was called by the IB guys to their office a few days after you returned. They confronted me with facts I never knew," he said.

He then began to narrate how the company generated untaxed money.

"The Juice Packaging Plants shipped approximately thirty percent of their product without proper documentation along with standard documented consignments to wholesale dealers across various states. These untaxed and unvouchered products were sold at regular prices without receipts by the retailers. The entire industry is complicit in this, with the tacit approval of taxation authorities. The taxes saved lead to increased profits shared by us, the dealers, and the retailers," he recounted. "We also benefit from savings on income tax. All of this is commonplace; it has become the norm. The cash flowed in from various dealers from all over India. I collected it and stored it in my safe at the office. Periodically, Mr. Khan would collect all of it and take it away for the boss."

I listened with rapt attention.

"After your abduction and escape, the IB began to suspect some connections between Mr. Khan and terrorist organizations. They quizzed me about this and the six cash transactions we had received. I told them that I simply kept the packages in the safe and handed them over to Mr. Khan when he requested them. I told them that Mr. Khan made trips each time after collecting this money. The IB agents seemed satisfied, but one can't fully trust them. I find myself in a bind and feel quite vulnerable," he concluded.

I asked Mr. Dubey to relax and enjoy the drinks.

"Mr. Khan is gone, and it will be difficult for law enforcement agencies to prove anything without him,"

I said, trying to reassure him. Moreover, you have cooperated with the IB, and they are only interested in getting information," I opined.

We ordered a second round of drinks, had lunch, and left the club late in the afternoon.

So, whatever Mr. Khanna had said turned out to be correct. Not only was the company giving monetary help to terrorist organizations, but it was also routing cash from foreign entities to these groups. Perhaps Farookh siphoned some of the cash to compensate himself for his own profits being given to the terrorists. I realized I was working for an anti-national organization. This was upsetting.

Weeks passed uneventfully. Mr. Dubey had yet to find a suitable job. Perhaps reassured by my earlier statement during lunch, he felt secure for the time being. In mid-July, I received another call from Khanna. It was rather unsettling to hear from him. After exchanging pleasantries, he informed me that Farookh was under pressure from the people in the valley who had not been receiving any funds from him lately. Intercepted conversations revealed that Farookh had communicated his inability to dispatch funds since Khan had died, and there was no one available to carry the cash. Khanna requested a meeting on Sunday, and I agreed.

I met Khanna at his dilapidated office on July 16th at eleven a.m.

"The callers from Kashmir," he began, "are threatening Farookh for not delivering the cash from his company and refusing to reroute the funds from abroad. Since Khan is unavailable for this, they are threatening to send their own people to collect the cash. Farookh was dissuading them from doing so."

He continued to inform me that sooner or later, someone would come to extort money from Farookh. He wanted Mr. Dubey and me to stay alert and notify him when the money has been collected and handed over to Farookh or someone else on his instructions. He further suggested that such people were enemies of the state and needed to be eliminated.

"Yes," I agreed.

"So, you wouldn't hesitate to do it?" he asked.

"No, I didn't mean that; I merely agreed with you," I defended.

He started to laugh.

"We know what you are capable of. We appreciate how you fared against the militants—or should we say, terrorists—during your escape," he said appreciatively.

"You did well with Khan as well," he added accusatorily.

"What do you mean?" I asked, shocked.

"Do you think we don't know?" he asked.

"I was at the 'Coffee Break' when Khan fell," I reminded him.

"Do you have a receipt to prove that?" asked Khanna.

I said, "Yes, I have it even now."

"Do you have any other receipts from the 'Coffee Break' with you?" he asked.

I knew I had fallen for his trap.

"No," I replied.

He started laughing again.

"Why save just this particular receipt?" he asked.

I was silent for a while.

"I hold onto the receipts for a few days," I lied.

But I knew he was onto me.

"Never mind that," he said seriously. "Please keep me informed. It's of national importance. We don't want you to be seen as an accomplice," he threatened.

I left his office in a very dejected mood.

I spoke with Mr. Dubey and conveyed the gist of my conversation with Khanna. I persuaded him to be on the right side of the law. I reminded him of his moral responsibility to the nation. He must also let Khanna know when the money is arranged.

Dubey was finally convinced. He now looked forward to the role he was to play in helping the law enforcement agencies.

On August 3rd, 2000, Indians received very disturbing news. It read as follows:

"NEW DELHI, Aug. 2 - *In a killing spree, shocking even for the bloodied mountains and forests of Kashmir, at least 93 people were slain late Tuesday and early today in six separate massacres.*

Most of the dead were innocent pilgrims on their way to pray at a holy shrine, labourers working at a brick kiln, villagers awakened from their beds and lined up for slaughter.

To many in India, the cause of all this murder seemed straightforward enough: a peace process begun last week by one militant group has been deemed a contemptible betrayal by others, requiring sabotage.

It is clear that after the Hizbul Mujahideen called for a cease-fire and talks, other militant groups have been instructed by Pakistan to step up their attacks on innocent and unarmed people, India's prime minister, Atal Behari Vajpayee, told the Parliament."

This news upset me. I had escaped, but so many others were not as fortunate. My company had contributed to this massacre by funding them. There was little anyone could do. Mr. Dubey also expressed his dismay over the tea we had together that day. He informed me that substantial cash had been received from the distributors. One or two more consignments, and it should be ready to be shifted. Armed with this information, I called up Khanna and gave him the input.

"We need to meet again," he urged.

I readily agreed, angered by the incidents in Kashmir.

An equally disturbing event had occurred in January of this year when 35 Sikhs from a single village called Chittisingpora in the Anantnag district of Kashmir were gunned down, leaving behind a village of widows and orphaned Sikh children.

Assassin

I informed Priya that I would be late. Khanna and I met that evening on the lawns near India Gate, selecting a secluded bench.

"I'm going to ask you to undertake a very challenging task for the security forces," he began. "We know you can do it," he said emphatically.

I held my breath and waited.

"You are going to take out Farookh," he stated in a very straightforward manner.

"No way!" I replied, shocked.

"You got rid of Khan, didn't you?" he said.

I remained silent as he outlined the plan.

"Soon, the extortionist from the valley will come to collect the funds. We are monitoring their phone conversations. When that happens, Farookh will have no choice but to deliver the cash consignment himself, and we will be aware of it. We plan to arrest the extortionists when they arrive in Delhi. With the advantage of knowing Kashmiri and your Kashmiri accent, you'll establish a collection point that I will choose for you. When Farookh arrives, you will collect the money and put two or three bullets into him and then escape in a getaway car that will be arranged for you. We will attribute his murder to Kashmiri extortionists, ensuring his image remains untarnished. Later, we will take care of the extortionists in our own way."

"Why not let them take the money and arrest everyone while the money was exchanging hands?" I asked Khanna.

"Farookh would plead his innocence and portray himself as a victim, claiming to be threatened by terrorists," Khanna explained. "The others would also hire lawyers and engage in a lengthy legal battle. If we don't involve you, the extortionists will dictate the location of the exchange, which is likely to be a public place. If they attempt to resist arrest, a shootout could ensue, endangering civilians. This would create a very ugly situation."

I was silent but I was beginning to see why this needed to be done this way.

"What if Farookh or others recognize me?" I asked.

"We will alter your appearance a bit. In any case, Farookh won't be there to tell," he summarized.

"I don't know how to use a handgun," I said.

"We know you are a quick learner. We will run some classes for you at the range," he answered, smiling.

I knew that I was being used and blackmailed to assassinate my own boss under the guise of doing my duty to the nation. But I was too deeply entangled in it now. "I will think about it," I said while rising to leave.

"You are a patriotic Kashmiri, and you have little choice," he said, praising and threatening me all at once.

We shook hands and parted.

August 12th and 13th

On August 12th, Khanna called me in the afternoon and asked me to come to his office at eleven the next day. As usual, it was a Sunday. Khanna was waiting for me in the parking lot, walking back and forth. We shook hands, and he led me to his car and invited me inside.

"How are things?" he asked as he drove out of the parking lot.

"Getting along," I replied.

We drove for about an hour, exchanging small talk and cursing the Delhi traffic. We arrived at a Police Unit Camp. After identification and registering in the visitor's log, we were permitted to enter. My name was not recorded. Khanna informed the guard that I was with him. We drove straight to a range. He retrieved a bag, and I followed Mr. Khanna. He pulled out a pistol and several magazines.

"This is a Beretta 9mm pistol with a capacity of fourteen rounds," he explained. "It's advisable to load ten rounds to maintain the spring's effectiveness."

He proceeded to explain its features, including safety. He mentioned that he wouldn't be giving me lessons on stripping and assembly. He set up a few targets approximately twenty feet away, loaded and cocked the weapon himself, and asked me to fire.

"The secret," he said, "was to squeeze the trigger like a lemon and let the pistol fire itself."

I went through two magazines quite deliberately. My accuracy was fairly good. Khanna didn't allow me to use both hands like they do in movies. After firing two magazines, he had me practice cocking the pistol repeatedly. I practiced chambering the round and decocking the hammer. A pistol can be fired either by pulling the trigger or by manually pulling the hammer back first and then pulling the trigger. The trigger is lighter in the second case and offers better accuracy. We approached the targets until we were merely eight to ten feet away.

He handed me the entire magazine and said, "Fire two rounds rapidly at the head, pause, and then at the chest in quick succession."

I loaded the magazine, cocked the pistol, decocked the hammer and brought the pistol alongside my thigh. I then raised it, pulled the hammer back and fired two rounds in quick succession into the target's head accurately.

"The chest!" shouted Khanna.

I aimed the weapon at the chest and fired two more rounds. They hit their mark as well. I repeated the exercise until the magazine ran out of bullets. I was given another magazine and made to repeat the exercise all over again.

"Your training is over for the day," said Khanna.

We headed to the Police Officers' Mess for some beer and lunch. I felt like a soldier.

"We may or may not have time for another practice," Khanna said over lunch.

We drove back to his office's parking lot, chatting idly. I picked up my car and returned home at five. Priya was annoyed with me. I had been going out for work most Sundays lately.

Three days later, Khanna called me to say that two extortionists were enroute to Delhi by train and planned to depart by road after collecting the money. They were expected to reach Delhi Station on the 17th of August by the Jhelum Express. That evening, Mr. Dubey informed me that sixty lakh rupees, equivalent to approximately one hundred and thirty-four thousand US dollars, had been taken home by Farookh in two large briefcases. I relayed this information to Khanna without specifying the amount. No one knew how much Farookh would hand over to the extortionists or how much he would reserve for future payments or other uses. I asked Khanna what would transpire if the money was collected from Farookh's home.

"Plan B," he replied.

He explained that they would then apprehend the extortionists with the money and proceed with legal action, which would result in a prolonged legal battle with an uncertain outcome. We have their photos, and they will be monitored. I hoped and prayed that Plan 'B' would come into effect, sparing me the ordeal.

August 17th

On 17th August, at about eleven am, Khanna informed me on the phone that the couriers had arrived. He further said that they are heading for the Pahar Ganj area, which has several budget hotels ensuring anonymity. About an hour later, I was informed that they had checked in at a hotel and that a raid to arrest them was being planned by the IB and Delhi Police. I began to feel nervous. I was on. I will be executing the IB Plan either this evening or tomorrow. My hands began to sweat at the thought of it all. Khanna asked me to meet him at his office at seven. I rang up Priya to tell her that I would be late again. I reached Khanna's office at seven. He informed me that the two couriers had been picked up and taken to a safe house instead of the Police Station. It's time for that call to Farookh now. We discussed what was to be said, how it was to be said and how to keep the conversation as brief as possible. The conversation would start with announcing who I was, stating the purpose and giving a location and time for collection with a polite warning to be punctual. I wrote the conversation in Kashmiri and rehearsed it several times in the presence of Khanna.

"You are good Ajay", said Khanna after a few runs.

He then picked up the phone. I had 'butterflies in my stomach' and I began to sweat profusely. Khanna put the phone back in its cradle.

"You can't be nervous", he said. "It's crucial that you sound calm. Just think in what condition would Rhea and

Rohan be today, if Farookh and Khan had succeeded, and you were killed and fed to dogs."

Anger began to replace anxiety. I almost became eager to square things up with these murderers.

"Call him", I said.

Khanna put on his headphones of the extension cord, handed me the handset and dialled Farookh's number. In barely three rings he answered.

"Hello", he said in a meek voice.

"*Salamawalekum* Mattoo *sahib*", I said.

"*Waalaikumasslam*", he answered.

"We have arrived and wish to collect the '*Zakat*' tomorrow and return in the evening", I said in a strong but polite tone.

"Come home and collect it," he said. "It will be safer, and I would be able to do *khidhmat* (serve you) as well", he offered.

Khanna and I both panicked. It was visible on both our faces.

"Your house could be watched, *janaab*", I said. "Why be so predictable?"

Khanna gave me a thumbs-up sign.

"Where then?", asked Farookh.

I gave him the address of a new multi-storied building near Faridabad and said, "basement car park".

"Will eleven be all right", I asked.

There was a pause.

"Make it twelve," he said. "I usually don't drive these days, but I will have to come alone in all that traffic", he explained.

"How will you explain this to your driver?", I asked him, out of the script.

"I'll send him with a small *zakat* to Jama Masjid tomorrow. I'll tell him that I need to brush up on my driving skills," he explained.

We exchanged greetings and hung up. Khanna and I shook hands in excitement at our first success.

Khanna ordered some tea.

"The basement car park would be empty except for a few intelligence personnel pretending to be common labourers putting the finishing touches on the new building," he explained over tea. "You'll leave your car at 'Shiv Properties' a few kilometres away and take your getaway car from there," he continued to instruct.

"You'll need to take a few hours off tomorrow to examine the upcoming apartments in the area," he suggested sarcastically.

"My tool?" I asked.

"It'll be there in the getaway car," he replied.

"What about my disguise?" I questioned.

He pulled out a packet from the table drawer. It contained a stooping moustache, the kind worn by stage performers. I looked at him in disbelief. He smiled and said it was enough to throw someone off the track.

As I got up, he said, "Pick up the money that Farookh brings and leave it in the getaway car when you leave. We need the money to nail the extortionists," he explained.

I drove home, anxious and in a sullen mood. I had been pushed into this quagmire by these political radicals and was now being sucked down further by the relentless sleuths. I promised myself this would be my last such act.

At home, I tried to act as cheerful as I could. I poured myself a large scotch and began chatting with Rohan and Rhea, for whom I had learned to survive and more. After dinner, I announced that I was very tired and needed to retire early for the evening.

"Alright, I understand," said Priya, teasing me.

The night was spent tossing and turning until Priya noticed and helped me divert my mind. I soon fell asleep.

August 18th

The morning was hot and humid, and clouds were gathering to signal a thunderous storm. I was perhaps quieter today because Priya noticed.

"Is everything okay at work?" she asked innocently.

"Yes," I said. It's just that I am now saddled with Yunus's workload as well without an assistant to help me. "

"Hire one soon. Farookh *sahib* has sanctioned the post", she advised.

I didn't answer that one. After a hurried breakfast, I headed to the office. I inquired with Mr. Farookh's office boy if the boss was in.

He answered, "Not yet." "He's likely to arrive late today," he informed me.

I went up to the HR head, Mr. Rastogi, and informed him that I had an appointment with a property agent to check out some upcoming apartments. I would be out for half a day, and I requested that he notify the boss if he asked for me. It was almost ten, and I needed to hurry. I took the elevator down to the car park basement and drove off to 'Shiv Properties'. It was well past eleven by the time I arrived. I realized I was late and that the whole plan could be jeopardized. I also considered being late on purpose to avoid the entire situation, but Khanna's wrath and subsequent consequences were even scarier.

I looked around for the getaway car. It was a white, inconspicuous Suzuki Zen parked a few spaces away. I opened the door and checked the glove box for the keys. The keys were there, along with a pistol and two magazines. Did Khanna expect me to have a pitched battle? I thought to myself. I put on my disguise, adjusting the moustache as best as I could, and looked into the rear-view mirror. Khanna was right; I couldn't recognize myself for a moment. I drove to a new building about ten minutes away, entered the basement car park, and reversed the car into a parking spot in take-off mode. There was no one in the basement. Two guys were loitering on the first floor, a little distance from the entrance to the car park. The wait was excruciating. I was nervous as hell; my heart was racing, and I couldn't bear to think that I was going to kill yet another man—a man I knew well and had worked for, for years.

To convince myself, I thought about my children and the many innocent people who had been murdered in Kashmir by the radicals. It was of little help. I decided to prepare. I inserted the magazine into the pistol, chambered a round, and decocked it, releasing the hammer. I will just have to pull the hammer back and shoot. No cumbersome cocking at the last moment giving the other guy time. By engaging in preparation, some of my nervousness receded. Where and how will I tuck in the pistol while approaching him? I had no idea. We hadn't thought of it, let alone practice it. I put the other magazine in my pocket just in case a gun battle ensued. The car park was empty. I got out and tucked the pistol into my belt behind my back. It felt comfortable and was easy to retrieve. I pulled the gun from its position a few times to ensure it was secure. I removed the pistol and sat back in the car, waiting. I didn't have to wait long.

I saw Farookh's Mitsubishi Lancer coming down the ramp very slowly. He was early, perhaps due to anxiety or because I had warned him to be punctual. He didn't see me in the car. He parked a few slots away, his car facing the wall, effectively trapping himself. I got out of my car, my heart pounding, tucked the pistol as I had practiced, and approached his car slowly. I came to the passenger side (left side in India) and knocked on the window. I heard a click and opened the door with my left hand while moving my right hand back to grip the pistol.

When the door opened wide enough, I drew the pistol and aimed it at Farookh, cocking the hammer. I was meant to shoot now without delay, but I couldn't bring myself to do it.

Farookh now recognized me, despite my moustache, and simply asked, "Why?" in Kashmiri.

"You tell me why," I responded, leaning into the car to speak more easily.

"I'm sorry I was under pressure," he said in Kashmiri.

"You were prepared to orphan my children and make Priya a widow." I reminded him in Kashmiri.

He began to shift in his seat and said, "Look, let me explain," while attempting to open his door, or so it seemed.

"I'm listening," I said.

Instead of the door opening, I saw him pull out a small revolver.

I was startled, as if I had suddenly encountered a cobra, and instinctively pulled the trigger three times in quick succession with my pistol. All three rounds hit Farookh in the chest. Farookh was able to fire once at me. I felt some heat on my left ear as the bullet whizzed past it. He tried to raise the revolver again, grunting. I leaned inside further, held his revolver down with my left hand and very calmly shot him in the head. His head hit the window as the glass shattered, and he slumped on the steering wheel.

I did not look at him again. I tucked the pistol back into my belt. I picked up the two briefcases from the passenger side of the car and walked back to mine. The briefcases were large and heavy. I placed them on the rear seat of my getaway car and drove off slowly to avoid attracting undue attention. I touched my left ear to check if I was bleeding. When I saw my hand, it only had some gunpowder residue. My anxiety had faded. I drove off normally.

Upon reaching 'Shiv Properties', I parked the getaway car next to mine. I placed the handgun and magazines back in the glove box and removed the car key to put it in there as well. After detaching my moustache, I exited the vehicle. I grabbed one of the briefcases and placed it in my car, locking it again before walking into the building. I was attended to immediately; while the sales executive greeted me, an attendant brought me some water. I took the glass and drank it quickly.

"It's very warm and humid outside," I remarked, explaining my thirst.

I asked if I could use the washroom and was guided to it. After relieving myself, I checked the mirror for any injuries or telltale marks. Upon returning, I sat down for a detailed briefing on the new apartments that were being developed, including their layouts, anticipated facilities, and payment plans. The air conditioning was pleasant and refreshing. Thirty minutes into the briefing, I began collecting the glossy brochures and assured them I would be in touch. I noted my address and home phone number in the customer register book and thanked them before heading out. The first thing I noticed was that the getaway car was gone. I returned to my office by half past two, waiting for news.

It was four when I received a call from Mehtab, hysterical and sobbing.

"Someone killed Farookh," she wailed. "Someone shot him," she continued. "I'm heading to Moolchand Hospital; please get there immediately."

"Yes, I'll be there," I replied.

It was my turn to spread the news to everyone. I started with Mr. Rastogi and then informed Mr. Dubey. Soon, everyone knew. "I'm headed to Moolchand Hospital," I almost shouted on my way out so that everyone would hear.

Before leaving, I asked a colleague to call my wife and Shyama to reach Moolchand Hospital. Mehtab would need all the support we could offer. As I went down in the elevator, I thought about the briefcase in my car and what to do with it while handling the situation at hand. I reached my car, a grey Maruti Suzuki 800, opened the hatch, and removed the cardboard cover and the spare wheel. I placed the briefcase in the cavity, covered it with the cardboard, and put the loose spare wheel on top, as if it had been changed in a hurry. Having done this in about five minutes, I drove off to the hospital.

At the hospital, Mehtab and Farookh's driver, who had gone to deliver *Zakat* to Jama Masjid earlier that morning, had just arrived. We entered the trauma centre. Five or six police officers were surrounding a wheeled stretcher. We approached it. "Mrs. Farookh Mattoo," I announced to the officers, and they stepped aside to allow her to reach the stretcher. A sheet covered the body, which bore some traces of blood. One officer restrained her from removing the sheet from the face. Looking at me, he asked, "Are you with her?"

"Yes," I replied.

"Be with her and hold her," he instructed.

I did just that, and he removed the sheet from the face. It was indeed Mr. Farookh. His head wound had been cleaned, but the face was distorted due to the impact of the bullet having gone through his skull. Mehtab saw this, and her legs buckled. She fainted. The police officer was experienced. I caught her, but she gradually sank to the floor. The nurses intervened. Water was sprinkled on her face. Some were rubbing her hands.

After a few minutes, she regained some consciousness. Dazed, she stayed on the floor, helped by nurses. She was offered water. She took a sip or two and then brushed the disposable container away. By this time, Shyama Khan, our new welfare officer, had arrived. They both hugged each other and wailed. It would have been a heart-wrenching sight for many. But I knew more. By now, Priya and some more colleagues from the office had reached the Trauma Centre, which was becoming crowded. The medical staff present instructed some of us to step outside.

Mehtab had regained some of her composure and sat in a chair provided by the nursing staff at the trauma centre. She accepted a hot coffee brought to her by someone. The Deputy Commissioner of Police (DCP) arrived, and there was a lot of saluting. He spoke briefly to an inspector and then turned to Mehtab.

He informed her that there would be formal identification and a postmortem. The postmortem was required to be conducted during daylight hours, so they had to hurry. A few police officers, some in plain clothes and others in uniform, began the documentation. Identification and a 'Panchnama' (a report signed by five witnesses) were completed. The DCP then requested Mehtab to leave. He informed her that the body would be released to the family by 10 AM tomorrow, and they could prepare for the funeral accordingly. All the women stood up and reluctantly started to leave. By now, Mehtab had regained her composure. Reconciled to what had happened, she was seen trying to wipe tears from Shyama's eyes, who had begun to weep inconsolably.

"Mr. Raina and Farookh *sahib*'s driver will report to the local police station," the DCP ordered. Mehtab had been driven to the hospital by her personal chauffeur. Farookh's driver had accompanied her after delivering the *Zakat* at the Jama Masjid. I was anxious. Soon, I, along with Farookh's stolen briefcase, would be just outside the police station.

At the police station, a junior Inspector asked me about my whereabouts during the day. I informed him that I had come to the office and taken a few hours off to explore some apartment options, contemplating acquiring one. I returned to the office in the afternoon.

"The time of your absence matches the time of the murder," said the man recording the statement.

I missed a beat, and my lips dried up. My pulse began to race. 'What if Khanna abandons me now after the dirty work has been done?' I thought. I couldn't implicate him, as I had no proof of his involvement. The briefcase I had stolen lay just a few meters away, enough to seal my fate.

"Do you have any proof that you were at the Shiv Properties?" he asked.

"Yes," I answered. "You could call them," I suggested.

I almost mentioned that I had their brochures in my car. The inspector and the man recording my statement began discussing the distance from the murder site to Shiv Properties. They concluded that it was about fifteen to twenty minutes, depending on traffic. Then they both looked at me. I thought my game was over.

"What is your position in the company?" the inspector inquired.

"Vice President of Administration," I replied.

"How was your relationship with the deceased?" he questioned.

"Very cordial," I answered. "He gave me a promotion a few weeks back," I added.

With no more questions, I was allowed to leave. I offered to stay, saying that I would drop off Farookh *sahib*'s driver after the questioning. The driver had also been interrogated at length, and we left the police station together.

"What was the focus of the questioning?" I asked him on our way back.

"They seemed to harp on the fact that perhaps Farookh *sahib* purposely wanted to go alone," he replied. "That's why he sent me on an errand," he concluded.

We remained silent for the rest of the journey. Upon reaching Farookh *sahib*'s home, I noticed a large crowd had gathered, all seated on the floor of the spacious and deep *veranda* on white sheets, as is customary in India during mourning. Some ladies were in the drawing room, where the furniture had been pushed back to create space for people to sit on the floor. I met Priya and asked her if the Mattoo children had been informed. She mentioned that Mansoor was expected to arrive in a few hours from Dehradun. Mansoor, thirteen, was studying at Doon School. His sister, Farhana, nineteen, was a student in America and was boarding a flight from New York in about an hour. She was likely to arrive by noon tomorrow. The burial was planned for five in the evening.

I made a few calls from the drawing room, arranging some light dinner for the relatives who would soon begin to arrive. I ordered a light breakfast for the morning guests at nine. After that, I went to the kitchen and instructed the staff to serve the food that would soon arrive from the hotel. Having done that, I approached Shyama and asked her who was handling the funeral arrangements. I was told that Mehtab's cousin was in touch with the local *Maulvi* (cleric), who would oversee all the arrangements. Satisfied, I found Mehtab and sat down next to her. I then drafted an obituary stating that the funeral would take place at five pm on 19th August and showed it to Mehtab. She deliberated over it. She asked me to add the names of some close relatives and gave me the go-ahead. I stood up and called one of my colleagues, dictating the text of the obituary to him and asking him to have it published in all prominent newspapers. Once that was done, I returned to sit beside Mehtab.

I sat with her for about ten more minutes. Then I went to the kitchen and asked one of the servants for three large garbage bags. I stepped outside to where many cars, including my hatchback, were parked. I lifted the hatch, removed the spare wheel, and laid it on the ground. Next, I removed the cardboard cover as well. I then transferred the entire amount of money, which I estimated to be around thirty lac rupees (over sixty-six thousand US dollars), from the briefcase into the bags. After that, I took out the empty briefcase and placed the three bags of money in the cavity where the spare wheel should be. I replaced the cover and set the spare wheel on top, then locked the car. I took the empty briefcase and walked back to the house. I walked confidently into Mr. Farookh's office library and placed the briefcase alongside some others. Glancing over my shoulder to ensure no one was around, I wiped the carrying handle with my handkerchief. I then walked into the kitchen and asked for some water, wondering if anyone had seen me putting the briefcase back. I hoped that, with so much happening, no one had noticed.

It was past ten when Mehtab signalled that Priya, and I could leave. She asked me to drop Shyama off at her place as well. On our way back, the conversation revolved around who could commit such a heinous act. The question of Farookh *sahib* venturing out without his driver also arose.

"Perhaps it's a business rivalry or an extortionist," I suggested, intending for the theory to spread.

After dropping Shyama off, we proceeded home. The children were asleep. It had been an incredibly hectic and exhausting day, to say the least. The anxious wait for action, the kill, and managing the aftermath were quite telling. Exhausted, I got into bed after a shower.

August 19th

I woke up early to be on time at Farookh's residence to assist Mehtab. While I was brewing my tea, the newspaper landed with a whack, thrown onto our balcony. I picked it up hastily to see what it said. The news was prominently featured on the front page, with the headline stating, *"Farookh Ahmed Mattoo, a prominent industrialist and businessman, had been shot and killed."*

The article went on to describe the location, the probable motive of extortion, and the fact that he managed to fire a round from his licensed revolver, possibly injuring one of the assailants. The paper also included his obituary. The obituary described him as "a loving father, a caring husband, a wonderful leader, an industrialist of repute, and a philanthropist." I got dressed. Priya was awake too. She made me some toast, fried eggs, and another cup of *chai*. I asked her to pick up Shyama and join Mehtab later in the morning.

I arrived at the Mattoo residence around eight. The guests who had come during the night were having tea and biscuits. The servants were preparing to serve breakfast, which the hotel would soon deliver. I removed my shoes and approached Mehtab, who was sitting quietly on the ground with a cushion supporting her back. I sat beside her.

"You look very tired," I remarked. "Why don't you take a nap before more mourners start to arrive?" I suggested.

"Yes, I will do that." "Please ensure that this event does not disrupt the functioning of the company," she instructed.

She got up and left. I sensed I might end up running this company for her. I felt elated at the prospect. I had to remind myself that it was too early for such assumptions and that I could still be arrested for murder. Around ten a.m., I called my bank manager and asked if I could rent a locker at his bank. He said he would need to check the availability and would let me know in about fifteen minutes. I occupied myself in receiving more mourners who were arriving every minute. After about twenty minutes, a servant approached and announced that the bank manager wanted to speak with me. I took the call in the main hall and was informed that a locker was available and had been reserved for me. I told the manager that I would arrive around eleven and asked him to have the paperwork ready, as I was tied up with the events.

"Yes, I understand," he said. "Please convey my condolences to Mrs. Mattoo," he added before hanging up.

I reached the bank a little before eleven, and having signed the paperwork, I took the key to the locker. I carried the three bags through a crowded bank to where the lockers were, hoping that no one would get too suspicious. I stuffed the money into the locker with some difficulty. It was safe for the time being. I did not intend to keep the money here for long.

I now proceeded to the hospital to be in time to receive the body. A few relatives and the company's employees were already there to assist with the collection and transport of Mr. Farookh's body. A hearse had been arranged to carry the body home and later to the burial site near Haus Khas, roughly a half-hour drive away from the house. The place had been informed, and some other relatives were overseeing the arrangements there. After some documentations and signatures, the body was collected and transported home. Upon arrival, the body was placed on the *veranda* for everyone to pay their respects. There was occasional wailing and weeping as new mourners arrived. His face was covered; it was not a sight that the faint-hearted could bear to see. Mansoor had arrived late at night from Dehradun, escorted by a Doon School employee, and sat next to his father's body. Priya and Shyama sat near Mehtab. Mehtab had regained her composure, but her grief was evident. She broke down into quiet sobs every time she met a mourner. I couldn't help but notice how beautiful and graceful she appeared even while grieving. The man in me was at his worst.

In the afternoon, Farhana arrived. The meeting of mother, son, and daughter was heart-wrenching. In the late afternoon, preparations for the '*Janaza*' were made, and the procession began to move towards the burial site amidst the wailing and weeping of the women who were to remain at home. After the prayers, the body was lowered into the grave, and Mansoor poured some earth, followed by others. After the burial, everyone began to disperse, some going to their homes and others returning to the Farookh residence.

I also returned to Farookh's house, or should I say Mehtab's home now. I oversaw some arrangements, and at around eight, Priya and I headed back home, dropping

Shyama off enroute. When we got home, the children were all excited.

"Did you see the television, Dad?" questioned Rohan.

"Why, what happened?" I asked.

"The killers of Farookh uncle were shot in an encounter at a car park," he said, excited and shocked. "One policeman was also injured," he added before I could respond.

I went to the living room where the TV was located. Breaking news was being reported, stating that a team from the Special Crime Branch was investigating the area of the murder of Farookh Ahmed Mattoo, who seemed to have injured one of the assailants. When they were spotted near the newly constructed building, they attempted to escape back to the car park where they had committed the crime, perhaps in hopes of getting a car to flee. When confronted, they opened fire with foreign automatic pistols, as if that made any difference. One police officer was injured in the initial gunfire. During the firefight, both terrorists were eliminated. One of them appeared to have suffered a recent wound to the left shoulder. Authorities recovered ten lakh rupees (over twenty-two thousand US dollars), along with two pistols, four magazines, and some rounds of ammunition from the scene. It seems that the murder of Farookh Ahmed was committed over insufficient extortion payments made to Kashmiri militants.

"I'll get myself a drink," I said, leaving for my minibar. I asked the children to turn off the TV, as we were very tired and needed some peace and quiet.

I felt a tremendous sense of relief when I poured myself some scotch and headed to the refrigerator for some soda and ice. The murder I had committed had been pinned on those two. I was now absolved of it. Even IB could never blackmail me about this ever again. Khanna and his partners had appropriated about twenty lakh rupees (the equivalent of over forty-five thousand US dollars). Of course, it would be shared with his superiors as well. I took my drink and settled onto the balcony. Priya brought me some nuts and sat down beside me. My sense of relief and the elation I was feeling must have been so evident that Priya noticed and said, "You seem so relieved and relaxed."

"Yes," I replied. "The day is over; I'm alive and enjoying scotch. Isn't that reason enough?" I had a sound sleep that night.

Linking extortion to Kashmiri militants would raise questions and tarnish the otherwise impeccable reputation of Mr. Farookh. However, it would likely be viewed with sympathy because anyone can fall victim to extortion and threats.

The next day, the papers featured the news of the encounter as prominent headlines. I woke up early and headed to Mehtab's house to see if she needed anything done before I went to the office. Mehtab was sitting on the lawn with some relatives, a few of whom were having tea.

She stood up to greet me, took me aside, and said, "Ajay, please manage the company for a few weeks until the legal issues related to death and succession are sorted out."

"Yes, Mehtab," I replied, leaving for the office. I was happy at the prospect of managing the company from now on. However, I would have to ensure that I didn't ruffle any feathers with my superiors. Therefore, I decided to use Mehtab's name to convey orders and seek suggestions from top management on running the business.

Mehtab Takes Over.

I was able to run the company on behalf of Mehtab while she was in mourning. It was a tightrope walk while passing on my instructions as directions from Mehtab. Gradually, everyone, including the senior lot, began to understand that I would be assisting Mehtab in running the company in a big way. They attributed this to the fact that we were both of Kashmiri descent. This suited me fine, as it made my job easy.

On Monday, September 26th, I received a call from Mehtab asking me to see her after lunch. I arrived at her home at three o'clock. The servant asked me to take a seat on the *veranda* and went to inform Mehtab of my arrival. It took her about five minutes to emerge from the main entrance of the house, where she greeted me warmly. I stood up, and she smiled, saying, "No, no, please sit down."

She was grace, charm, and beauty all rolled into one person. She ordered some tea and instructed the servant to bring the walnut cake she had baked. Once the servant left, she opened the conversation.

"My forty days of mourning end on the 28th. I'd like to assume responsibility for the company on the 29th and will be attending the office that day," she said. "Please ask Mr. Dubey and Mr. Rastogi to brief me for about an hour. They can give me a presentation if they feel more comfortable," she added.

My heart sank. So, my hopes of running the company were merely a bubble after all.

"Yes, Mrs. Mattoo," I answered.

"What happened to Mehtab?" she asked, laughing.

"You're my boss," I replied.

"Very well, Mrs. Mattoo, it shall be," she acknowledged. "Ask the Plant GMs to brief me on the phone for about fifteen minutes each. Tell them I'll be visiting the plants sometime next month."

The tea was brought, and she poured a cup for me, adding half a spoon of sugar without asking. She knew how much sugar I liked in my tea. The cake was delicious. She informed me that all legal aspects of the succession of properties and the business had been completed by the family lawyers. This process was relatively straightforward since Farookh's Will was simple and clear, with no other claimants. The children were to be equal owners of the house and the business after Mehtab's demise. Serious matters behind us, small talk ensued, including discussions about the garden and what flowers were planned for the winter. It let me know that she was on the path of overcoming her grief. An hour had passed.

"Anything else, Mrs. Mattoo?" I asked, getting up.

"Yes, don't forget Mehtab," she smiled.

I smiled back, turned, and descended the few steps from the *veranda* to where my car was parked.

"You need a new car," I heard Mehtab call after me.

I turned back.

"I'll work towards it," I yelled in reply.

My happiness returned. Things weren't as bad as I had thought.

Back in the office, I informed Mr. Rastogi and Mr. Dubey of Mrs. Mattoo's plan to attend the office on the 29th and the requirement to brief her. I also rang the Plant GMs about the phone calls they needed to make and the new MD's likely visits to the plants.

I then went into the MD's office and inspected it. I gave the office boy the necessary instructions to spruce up the office. I pointed out a few things and said that I would inspect it again on the 28th. At 5:30 p.m., I left the office, thinking about which car to buy.

On September 28th, the office appeared neater than usual. Everyone had worked to tidy up and organize their desks. The restrooms were cleaner, the elevator gleamed, and the cafeteria also seemed more inviting. Some flowers had been placed in the MD's office, which had been cleaned without disturbing Mr. Farookh's drawers and personal belongings. It would be up to Mrs. Mattoo to handle that. There was a debate among senior members of the office about whether to welcome her with flowers, considering the circumstances of her assuming office. It was decided that just one bouquet would be presented to her upon arrival by a female employee.

On September 29th, at ten o'clock, I went down to the car park and waited. Her car, driven by her chauffeur, arrived at a quarter past ten.

"Good morning," I said as I opened her door.

"Hello," she replied, extending her hand towards me.

We shook hands, and I escorted her to the elevator.

As the elevator ascended, she mentioned, "I need to meet everyone this week. "

"We will organize that," I responded.

At her office, she was welcomed by the lady designated to present her with a bouquet, Mr. Dubey and Mr. Rastogi. She shook hands with everyone. The peon opened the door; she thanked him and entered the office. We noticed her becoming tearful. She composed herself, dabbed her eyes, and sat down in the chair.

"Can you leave me alone for a few moments, please?" she asked in Hindi.

We all left and returned to our respective cabins.

She must have spent about ten minutes alone, after which she called her office boy, Manohar and spent the next ten minutes or so with him. She then called for me and asked me to introduce the staff to her. We descended to the fourth floor, where I introduced everyone. She shook hands with some and nodded at others, some of whom had met her earlier on various occasions. We then went up to the fifth floor again, where she met everyone there except Mr. Rastogi and Mr. Dubey. We proceeded to the Conference Room, and the briefings commenced with Mr. Dubey leading the first one. The briefings concluded by three in the afternoon. Mehtab expressed her desire to leave, and I escorted her to her car.

"Will you be doing this every day?" she asked.

"If you wish me to," I answered.

"No, let Manohar do it," she instructed.

She got into the car and left. I returned to my cabin and ordered some coffee.

Mehtab's routine involved attending the office five days a week. She would arrive by eleven, sign cheques and authorizations, and make decisions that required her intervention. Occasionally, she spoke with the plant GMs on the phone to authorize major transactions or maintenance work that necessitated unusually high expenditure. Every second Monday, she sought presentations from the CFO and the HR head. Her leadership style was participatory, with minimal interference until she noticed something concerning. The team was performing well, and the business was thriving. This period marked a shift as Indians moved away from unhealthy carbonated drinks and began opting for fruit juices instead. Fuelled by increased purchasing power and promotions on TV channels, these juices became a popular choice among the middle class as well. Despite her busy schedule, Mehtab had plenty of time for Mahjong, Bridge, and occasional ladies' club parties.

In the second week of October, Mehtab called for a conference with all the plant GMs, CFO, HR head, the newly appointed Company Secretary, and me. Arrangements for the conference and the accommodations for the GMs were made at the Taj Hotel, as it was close to the Mattoo residence. The Plant GMs, accompanied by their wives, were to arrive by the afternoon of the 12th. A dinner was arranged that evening at the hotel, which was to be attended by the heads of the local office, the three Plant GMs and their wives, and Mehtab. The conference was scheduled for the 13th in one of the hotel's conference halls, followed by a working lunch. Mehtab was hosting a dinner that evening at her residence for all attendees and their spouses. The GMs would be free to return on the 14th, but they could spend a few additional days in Delhi or elsewhere if they wished before returning. My hands were full of arrangements to be made for the upcoming conference.

The atmosphere during the dinner on October 12th was more introductory and less formal. Mehtab was meeting the Plant GMs and their wives for the first time after taking over as MD. She had, of course, met them as Mrs. Mattoo on earlier occasions. It was about eleven when the dinner concluded, and I escorted Mehtab to the lobby while waiting for her car. She looked as graceful as ever. I felt self-conscious as a few hotel guests in the lobby stole glances at us. The car arrived at the porch. She sat down and rolled down the window, extending her hand out of it. I took it gently.

"Thank you, Ajay," she said.

"Good night, Mehtab," I replied.

She smiled as the car rolled forward, her smile stirring something in me once more.

The conference next morning was quite formal, with various details and data that some, including Mehtab, may not have fully understood. However, it was clear that the business was thriving. Profits of both kinds were being generated to warrant expansion. A decision was made to explore the possibility of establishing a plant in the grape-growing region of Maharashtra, near Shirdi or Nasik. We discussed capacity enhancement for the existing plants at length. After the lunch break, Mehtab approached me and mentioned that she wanted me to visit the Mattoo residence to check on the dinner arrangements and see if the household staff needed any assistance. I left the hotel, and upon arriving at the Mattoo residence, everything appeared to be well in control. The head servant informed me that they had successfully managed numerous such dinners before. The kitchen staff was also busy and handling everything efficiently. I wondered why I was sent. I returned to the hotel an hour later to participate in the remaining meeting. As I joined the discussion, I sensed that I was drawing slightly more attention from everyone than usual. Just my imagination, I thought.

The conference concluded around four o'clock. Mehtab expressed her gratitude to everyone for their participation, stating that the company's success rested in their hands. She admitted to knowing very little and relied on the team's support.

Finally, she said, "Let me congratulate Ajay on his promotion to President."

I was taken aback. There was some applause and smiles. As we dispersed, congratulations echoed around. I had picked up two promotions within a year and was now at par with other departmental heads. I escorted Mehtab to the car once more.

Before she got in, she smiled and asked, "Happy?"

"Thank you, Mehtab," I replied, looking sombre.

"Cheer up," she added patting my arm lightly before entering the vehicle. After seeing Mehtab off, I hurried back to the hotel lobby and asked for the phone. I called Priya to share the good news.

Everyone arrived for dinner at around seven. Mehtab was on the lawns to greet everyone personally. Dressed in a maroon and black chiffon sari, she looked stunning. Her signature bun added elegance to her five-foot five-inch lithe frame. She appeared taller in her outdoor heels. She congratulated Priya on my promotion, and Priya thanked her.

"You look gorgeous," Priya said, marvelling at her poise.

Mehtab burst into laughter and replied, "thank you." "You're looking quite charming yourself," she added, playfully pinching Priya's cheek.

Drinks and snacks were being served on the lawns, which had ample seating. Soon, the sounds of alcoholic banter filled the air, accompanied by laughter here and there. The ladies chose to sit while the gentlemen moved about. Mehtab seemed to be everywhere, interacting with everyone somehow. The pleasant October breeze enhanced the atmosphere. The weather was ideal for outdoor gatherings.

After greeting the other guests, she returned to the group of ladies where Priya was. Mehtab took my elbow gently as she guided me along.

"I have a confession to make," Mehtab said, addressing Priya again.

Priya became a little apprehensive.

"I'm going to saddle Ajay with a lot," she declared. "I hope you'll bear with it," she added apologetically.

"You can saddle him as much as you want, as long as he brings in the *moolah*," Priya said with a giggle.

Mehtab threw her head back and laughed, turning slightly red before covering her mouth and glancing at me. I merely smiled uneasily. Priya also felt a touch embarrassed by what she had just said but laughed it off. I excused myself and walked away, pretending to get a drink. Mehtab's laughter and her looks were immensely suggestive. I could feel my heart racing.

The dinner was a sit-down affair on the *veranda*. Three tables seating four each had been laid out, along with one table for eight. It was a buffet with a service table managed by servants near the dining room. The three Plant GMs and their wives were seated at the larger table, with Mehtab at the head. One chair remained unoccupied. The others dined at the three smaller tables, with a few extra spaces scattered about. The menu was superb, featuring fish mayonnaise, shredded grilled chicken, and Russian salad as the main dishes, accompanied by impressive side dishes. Various types of bread from the renowned Wenger's of Connaught Place were available in different baskets. It was an old-school charming outdoor dinner, with attendants scurrying about offering more helpings of the dishes right at the tables. Desserts ranging from soufflés to caramel custard to ice cream were served at the tables. Most guests enjoyed wine with their meals. A dedicated servant with a trolley was going around refilling the wine glasses with guests' preferred selections. The dinner was truly a fabulous affair. Occasionally, someone would peek from the *veranda* on the first floor, occupied by Omar Ahmed Mattoo and his wife, the younger sibling of Farookh. Their daughter was studying in Canada. They hadn't been invited, perhaps because it was a professional gathering, or maybe due to the estrangement that often occurs among wealthy siblings.

The dinner wrapped up around midnight, and Priya and I were the last to leave. Mehtab escorted us to our car.

"Ajay needs a new car," Mehtab mentioned once more.

We drove home, discussing the wonderful hospitality and which car to purchase. We decided to go look for one next Sunday. In India, our choices were limited in the year 2000, and we were most likely to afford a Suzuki Esteem.

The next day, during office hours, I received a call from Mehtab. It was very unlike her to call on a Saturday, and she seemed disturbed. She proceeded to tell me that she had received a legal notice in which Omar Mattoo was contesting her claim to the entire business, stating that family wealth had been used to create the business and that he had a stake in it as a sibling. She went on to tell me that she had consulted her lawyer before calling me, and he assured her that there was nothing Omar could claim legally. However, he could initiate lengthy litigation and become a nuisance.

"If he can be a nuisance, so can we," I said instinctively. There was a moment of silence on the phone. "How is he occupying part of your house?" I asked Mehtab.

"It's been willed to him," she replied.

I urged her to relax. "I will look into it," I said.

"All right," she sighed before hanging up.

I called Khanna at his office. He answered after several rings. I announced myself.

"Oh well! It's Ajay," he said almost mockingly. "You seem to have vanished," he accused me in Hindi, laughing.

"Well, yes, I wanted to get away from it all," I answered apologetically.

"What is it?" he asked in Hindi.

"I need a background check on Omar Ahmed Mattoo," I said, getting straight to the point. "He is Farookh's younger brother," I added.

"Why?" Khanna asked.

"He also appears to have connections with terrorists or militants, or however you might want to refer to them," I explained.

"Why does it 'seem' so to you?" he questioned, emphasizing the word 'seem'.

I hesitated for a moment.

"He is a Kashmiri Muslim. His brother was a confirmed supporter of the separatists. He is also likely involved, in all probability," I stated, unconvincingly.

"Is it patriotism talking or could there be another motive?" he asked.

I fell silent.

"Never mind that question," he continued. "I'll ask Mathur to have his background checked and will get back to you in about two weeks," he assured me. "Your assumption has its reasons, you know," he added. "It could lead us to something; one never knows," he concluded.

"Thank you so much," I replied.

"Oh! You're welcome," he said before hanging up.

Sunday, 15th October, was an exciting day for the family. We were all heading to the local Suzuki showroom to select our new car. Sundays were usually relaxed with a late, leisurely, and hearty breakfast, but not today. This Sunday was different. Everyone was up and dressed on time. The breakfast was a quick affair, featuring discussions about the possible colour of the car. I had to remind the children that the showrooms opened at eleven, and we couldn't arrive while the janitor was still cleaning up. The family's mood was festive.

At the showroom, Rohan and Rhea were in and out of every car that was shown to us. The Zen was too small, the Baleno was different and expensive, and the Esteem (a foregone conclusion) seemed right for us. What remained was the selection of the colour. It came down to silver, Rohan's choice, versus white, which was preferred by Rhea and Priya. The salesman had to resort to a flip of a coin to ascertain that Rhea and Priya would soon get their white Esteem. With the cost negotiated, the advance was paid in cash, and the sales executive assured us that 'our' car would be delivered on the 25th of October, a day before Diwali. Instead of going home after the deal, we went to Karim's at Green Park for a Mughlai lunch. It had been an enjoyable day for all of us. While we waited for someone to take our order, I held Priya's hand and kissed it in public view. The children felt embarrassed and giggly. They only stopped when the waiter arrived to take the order. The lunch was delicious. We returned home late in the afternoon. I turned in for a nap.

The start of the next week was normal. Mehtab was briefed by Rastogi and Dubey. She didn't seem overly anxious about the litigation her brother-in-law had threatened her with. Her lawyer appeared to have reassured her. After the briefing, she asked me to prepare an itinerary for her visits to the plants. We could begin with the Shillong Plant after Diwali. The prospect of 'we' intrigued me.

I proposed the visit to Shillong from the 29th to the 31st of October, with plans for the Himachal plants in mid-November. For the Shillong visit, we would fly to Guwahati and then travel by road to Shillong. We would visit the plant the next day and return to Delhi via Guwahati on the 31st of October.

Scared Omar Mattoo

On the 19th at around three in the afternoon, I received a call from Khanna. He informed me that my suspicion was correct. Omar was also involved in receiving money from abroad by over-invoicing the Kashmiri carpets he exported and sending a portion of the extra profits to militants in Kashmir. The value of exported carpets and the business turnover mismatched considerably. Omar was also receiving funds through '*Hawala*,' a system of 'off the record' underground banking that organizations used to send money to militants. He had been siphoning off large sums before sending the rest to the carpet manufacturer for onward delivery. Tracing and questioning Omar's carpet suppliers was not difficult. The information came tumbling out.

"We will make a hoax call to him, pretending to be from the militant organization, to further confirm his involvement," he said. "We might order him to visit Sopore, masquerading as militant handlers," he laughed. "I'm sure by now Omar has been informed by the carpet manufacturers and suppliers that IB sleuths were asking questions about him."

I thanked him, and he in turn thanked me for the lead.

Khanna had delivered results well in time. Now, it was a matter of how to utilize the information. I would have to wait to see Omar and his wife's reaction for a few days or weeks. Fortunately, I didn't have to wait long. Mehtab called me to her chamber first thing the next day and asked if I had acted on the Omar matter in any way. I inquired why she was asking. She told me there had been quite the commotion in the Omar household last night, with shouting and counter-shouting between him and his wife.

"And why do you think it's because of me?" I asked.

"Omar came down in the morning and asked me for your number," she replied.

"Let him contact me, and we shall see what he wants," I said, smiling.

An hour later, I received a call from Omar. He wanted to meet me and invited me to the Gymkhana Club at three in the afternoon. Perhaps it was quieter then. I rang Mehtab and informed her of my scheduled meeting with Omar at three.

"Things are happening really fast," she said, sounding surprised.

"I will brief you later," I said.

I'll be waiting," she said and hung up.

I left the office at lunchtime for the Gymkhana Club, a highly sought-after and prestigious club in Delhi, built in the 1930s. I arrived a little after three. Omar was waiting at the reception, and we shook hands.

"Thanks for coming on such short notice," he said apologetically. He led me to a secluded spot. "What would you like?" he asked while also signalling for the waiter's attention. "Beer or gin and tonic?" he inquired.

"I would prefer tea with any snack that the Gymkhana boasts about", I replied.

The waiter arrived, and Omar ordered tea along with mutton cutlets. He then waited for the waiter to leave.

"I believe you were abducted in Kashmir," he started.

"Yes, sir, I was abducted when I had gone to Sopore to see if we could acquire some land for another plant," I replied.

"But they let you go?" he questioned.

"No, I escaped," I replied.

"How?" he asked.

"It's a long story. I'll have to write a book about it," I parried the question. He fell silent for a few moments. "What is it, Mr. Omar?" I asked him. He then began to speak.

He mentioned that he needed to travel to Kashmir for business to negotiate the prices of the carpets he exported. After learning about my ordeal, he was a bit apprehensive.

"What should I do?" he asked.

"Negotiate on the phone", I suggested nonchalantly.

He thought for a moment and said that he must see the material on offer to negotiate.

"Then you should go," I suggested. "You're a Kashmiri Muslim; you have nothing to fear," I said.

The waiter arrived and put two glasses of water on the table while we waited for the order.

"They killed Farookh despite him being a Kashmiri Muslim." "I wish I could wind up my business here and move out of the country," he said.

"You could consider that", I prompted.

"It means starting all over again," he moaned. "Where do I get the resources to do that?" he grumbled.

"You could become an importer of carpets in any country you choose to settle in," I suggested. "You have the knowledge and acumen, and you could import carpets from all over the world, not just Kashmir," I said, quite surprised at myself for this sudden idea.

Omar's eyes sparkled at the idea. "You are brilliant," he said, flattering me. "The problem is the resources needed to get started. Acquiring a house and launching everything requires a lot," he added.

The waiters arrived with our tea and a large platter of mutton cutlets. One laid out the teacups, plates, and cutlery, while a second waiter placed the tea set and the platter of cutlets on the table. Omar waited for the waiters to leave before offering me the cutlets. I was hungry, so I took two of them with some sauce. Omar served himself as well.

"You know, you can manage the resources you need," I said while eating. Omar paused chewing for a moment.

"How?" he asked.

"Sell your share of the house and any commercial property you own," I suggested, trying to convince him to leave India altogether and leave Mehtab alone.

He then went on to explain that his father's will prohibits the sale of the floor outside the family. "You could offer to sell it to Mehtab," I suggested.

"Does she have the resources to acquire it?" he asked.

"I don't know," I replied. "I'm having this conversation without her consent, you know. I'm merely putting forth an idea as a possible solution to your problem," I said.

He set his plate down and began pouring tea for both of us. He was thinking hard.

"Sir, discuss the idea with your wife, and if you both feel comfortable, I could then open the discussion with Mehtab about the proposal," I offered over tea. "It's a family issue and can be discussed freely at home," I added.

"Our relations haven't been very cordial," Omar said hesitantly.

"Well, I could mediate if you'd like," I offered. "But I should be going now," I said, setting my cup down.

Omar also stood up and accompanied me to the porch.

"I will get back to you," Omar said, shaking my hand.

I went back to the office and called Mehtab. I briefly explained what Omar and I had discussed and advised her not to show any eagerness. I also suggested that my plan was to establish a five-year deferred payment agreement with Omar. A substantial lump sum, comprising both legitimate and illegitimate funds, could be arranged for him to settle abroad, while the remainder could be paid in instalments.

"How did you manage it so soon?" she asked.

"The Almighty does it," I replied.

"I could hug you, you know," she said.

I didn't respond.

"Thank you, Ajay. I don't know what I would do without you," she said before hanging up.

I felt pleased about what I had accomplished. On my way home, I picked up some pastries for Priya and the kids.

Finally, it was October 25th. I took a day off work. The family was all excited, and we headed to the showroom around eleven in a taxi. After much fanfare, the 'Esteem' was handed over to us. The children's faces were glowing with happiness. We first drove to the nearest temple to have the car blessed, then returned home after picking up some '*ladoo*' sweets to celebrate. That evening, we went for a long, aimless pleasure drive beyond Faridabad. We enjoyed a rustic dinner at a '*Dhaba*,' an outdoor eatery, and returned home late at night.

The next day was Diwali, our first Diwali celebration in the new rented apartment. There was plenty of visiting and distribution of sweets and gifts. Many visitors also stopped by. We plugged in decorative lights along with traditional ghee lamps. As the sun set, fireworks lit up the city. The children too were outside on the street below, bursting crackers and sending rockets up into the sky. It was a joyous day, and everything had turned around for the family.

Early the next morning, while I was having my tea, I received a call from Omar. It was a sign of his anxiety that he couldn't wait for a reasonable hour to call me. He had likely waited all Diwali night to reach out first thing in the morning. After exchanging some pleasantries, he got straight to the point. He wanted to discuss the proposal to sell his portion of the house to Mehtab. He gave me the go-ahead and quoted an outrageous price for it. That was understandable, as further negotiations would likely lead to a more reasonable figure.

At the office, I waited for Mehtab to arrive. She showed up a few minutes past eleven. I gave her about half an hour to sort out her work. I called her on the internal office phone and asked if I could see her. She told me to come right away. When I entered her office, she was busy signing some cheques. She gestured for me to sit.

"Yes, Ajay," she said, putting down the pen and pushing the cheque books aside.

I recounted the conversation I had with Omar over the phone that morning. I advised her once more not to appear too eager. In the meantime, she should consult some property agents to determine a fair value for the property so we could establish our negotiating grounds.

She interrupted me.

"I'm doing nothing of the sort," she insisted. "It's you who will see this through," she almost commanded.

After consulting a few agents over the next two days, I estimated that Omar's share of the house would be valued at around sixty to seventy million rupees, or six to seven crores, as Indians would say. At that time, this was equivalent to approximately one and a quarter to one and a half million US dollars, sufficient for Omar to settle abroad and start his new import business.

Early on the morning of 29th October, when Mehtab and I were scheduled to fly to Guwahati for our visit to the Shillong plant, I received another call from Omar. He wanted to know if I had brought up the subject with Mehtab.

"No, not yet. Should I drop it?" I replied.

"No, not at all. I just wanted to find out if you've discussed the issue with her or not," he answered. "I'm in no rush," he lied. I guessed he was having sleepless nights.

"We will be out for a plant visit for the next three days. I will speak to her after we return," I said.

"Thank you," he said, sounding dejected.

The Visit

I reached the airport a little early to receive Mehtab and help her check in. She arrived barely forty-five minutes before the flight, just when I was beginning to get anxious. As business class passengers, we got priority, and we were able to board the flight well in time. Since the time was short, Mehtab and I did not have time to discuss things at the airport.

We were seated together, with Mehtab taking the window seat. The flight was scheduled to depart at noon and was almost on time. I could smell her wonderful perfume and couldn't help but notice her lovely arms and manicured hands so close to me. Our shoulders brushed while we fastened our seat belts. It felt good. The hostess walked past us a few times, smiling at us with her eyes wide in awe as she looked at Mehtab. I too received a special glance, being the 'lucky man' seated next to her.

After the flight took off, Mehtab said, "Say something,"

I hesitated. I wanted to say, "You smell wonderful." I refrained. "Omar called early this morning," I said. "He wanted to know if I had broached the subject of you buying the floor," I continued.

"So?" she inquired.

"I said no, not yet," I replied. "Let him sweat a little," I added.

The beverages and snacks were wheeled in, interrupting our conversation. Mehtab declined the refreshments. I acted greedily and took a Coke and the snack tray.

"Ajay, that was a brilliant masterstroke you pulled off," she said after the hostess had passed us. "I couldn't have asked for more from the Almighty. If I can acquire the first floor, the entire bungalow will belong to me and my children," she continued. "When Mansoor gets married, he can live on the first floor as long as I'm alive. We'll be together but still have our own space. Can we manage the funds to buy it?" she asked.

"With a deferred payment plan, we could," I replied.

She nodded, yawning. "I think I'll take a nap," Mehtab said. She lowered the window shutter, leaned her head against it, and closed her eyes. I began to relax in my seat while enjoying my meal.

We landed a few minutes past three and were greeted by a mid-level employee from the Shillong Plant, who drove us to our hotel. The three-hour journey through the mesmerizing hills was stunning.

"Lovely, isn't it?" Mehtab said several times.

"Yes," was my brief reply each time.

I was enjoying being next to her more than the hills of Shillong.

The Juicing and Packaging units were not particularly large. These did not have integrated guest rooms on their premises. They served solely as juicing and packaging facilities. Even the Plant GM resided off-site in a hired bungalow that sprawled across an acre of land. At that time, Shillong did not have any five-star hotels, so we were booked into the Tripura Castle, a heritage property originally constructed for the Tripura Royalty. It featured comfortable rooms and cottages filled with old-world charm and hospitality, located on the outskirts of Shillong amidst the pine forest. Mehtab had an independent cottage for herself, while I was assigned one of the deluxe rooms in the Forest Wing. We were invited by Mr. Tarun Baruah, the Plant GM, and his wife Teji Baruah, for dinner at their home. We had about two hours to freshen up before we would be escorted to the Baruah residence.

The Baruah residence was a sprawling bungalow, exuding the charm of an old English-style estate. The dinner was held indoors since Sikkim often experienced unannounced torrential rains. Two more couples, also top officials from the plant, were invited. Mehtab, dressed in a silk sari and looking her charming best as always, was relishing her new status and the attention she was receiving. She enjoyed her wine along with the occasional snack. She was chirpy and quick to laugh. The dinner was a sit-down affair set around a large dining table in a separate dining room. The continental food served by the two attendants was superb, complemented by wine throughout the meal.

While we were having dinner, it began to rain outside. Its intensity increased gradually as the evening progressed. The sound of the rain on the tin roof was wonderful. We had to raise our voices a bit to converse. Once dinner was over, it was time for some Cognac. It was well past eleven when Mehtab asked the hosts if she could leave. The car pulled up onto the porch, and we both got in.

"What fun," said Mehtab just as we drove out of the bungalow. "I could never have been so pampered if Farookh had been around," she added. I remained silent. The car was being driven rather slowly due to the rain and the curves. "Say something, will you?" she asked, pretending to be angry.

"You were looking gorgeous", I said.

"What do you mean by 'were' looking gorgeous?" she asked.

"You are gorgeous", I corrected myself.

She broke into soft laughter. Sitting so close, rubbing my shoulder and her flirtatious behaviour were becoming too much for me to bear.

"I must say, you enjoy your wine too", I added.

"Sometimes, when I'm in the mood," she replied.

The car arrived at the hotel and drove us to her cottage. The driver got out and opened an umbrella before he opened the door for Mehtab. I also got out from the other side and headed towards her. Mehtab took the umbrella from the driver and handed it to me. She thanked the driver, indicating he could leave. The driver rushed back into the car and drove off. I escorted Mehtab with the umbrella about fifteen paces to her cottage. We were so close that I could not merely smell her perfume but feel it too. In my attempt to stay a little away from her, my back was getting drenched. Under the portico, I set the umbrella on the ground. Mehtab opened the door and asked me to come in. She hurried towards the bathroom while I stood there, unsure of what to do. A moment later, the bathroom door opened, and she threw a towel at me.

"Dry yourself," she shouted. I couldn't help but notice her beautiful arm when she tossed the towel at me, as I began to wipe the water off.

"Heat up some water for coffee, will you?" she yelled from the bathroom.

I walked over to the kettle, poured in some water, and plugged it in. She emerged in a bathrobe, her hair loose and a considerable portion of her lovely legs showing.

"What a fun day," she said, coming close to me and slapping my hand.

I put my hand around her waist and pulled her closer. She didn't seem surprised. I held her face and gave her a long kiss. She responded in equal measure. We fumbled around, trying to switch off some of the lights. We were locked in this passionate kiss while trotting around, locked into each other. I undid her bathrobe to find an exquisite woman, beautiful and flawless. If there was a flaw, it only enhanced her sensuality. We tore into each other with hunger. What followed was pure lust. We were as shameless as animals. The kettle had boiled the water and switched itself off. We did not notice. We were on fire. Spent, we remained in bed with embers of lust still glowing. It was well past three when Mehtab asked me to go to my room, pushing me away. I put on some clothes, gathered the rest, kissed her again and walked out smiling to myself. What an evening it had been.

We met for breakfast at the restaurant at nine, as if nothing had happened the previous night. After a quick breakfast, we were driven to the plant where Mr. Baruah was waiting to receive Mehtab. Following a two-hour presentation that emphasized the need to expand and upgrade the packaging machines, we were taken on a tour of the plant. The plant was well run, with safety and hygiene measures in place. Mehtab was impressed and did not hesitate to express it. Mr. Baruah relished the compliments. A lunch was organized with all the supervisory staff at 2 PM, allowing Mehtab to interact with them. Some congratulated her on becoming the new MD, while others offered condolences for the passing of Mr. Farookh. The lunch was catered, and the staff enjoyed the lavish menu. The accounts briefing took place in the afternoon, after which Mehtab was shown the crèche, often visited by Mrs. Shyama Khan as the Welfare Officer. The plant operated two eight-hour shifts: the first from 7 AM to 3 PM and the second from 3 PM to 11 PM. Today, the plant ended the first shift half an hour early and started the second shift half an hour late. A grand high tea was organized by the plant for everyone, including the labour force. It was quite festive. Mehtab went around meeting everyone, asking them questions and inquiring about any problems they had. A member of the staff followed her, noting any grievances that were expressed. Everyone was in awe of her. Here again, some congratulated her while others condoled the passing of *'janaab'* Farookh. I marvelled at Mehtab's grace; she could make a great politician.

We returned to Tripura Castle well past five. Mehtab said she was tired and would have dinner in her cottage. Just as she was entering her room, she turned around and said, "Join me at nine."

I returned to my room, brewed some tea, and sat down on the balcony, contemplating and enjoying the forest. I was tired, too, so I took a nap for about an hour. I got up at eight, shaved, took a long shower, and went out for dinner at the cottage.

Dressed casually, with her hair in a ponytail, Mehtab looked different and great. She welcomed me in and asked what I would like. I opted for a large scotch with soda, and she poured herself some wine as we settled down.

"What a day!" Mehtab said. "I've never felt this important," she continued.

"You were great," I added.

"The plant is in safe hands and is being run very well," she remarked appreciatively.

"Mr. Farookh made a wise choice in selecting his plant heads," I suggested.

She didn't respond to that. Soon, dinner arrived with appetizers on a trolley. Mehtab instructed the staff to leave the plates until morning. My heart raced in anticipation as I saw the food trolley filled with a large platter of various kinds of Kababs, a salad platter with two types of dips, and dinner served in about four warm casseroles. Two wedges of mud cake rested on a small plate covered with a cloche. The Kababs were excellent. I walked over to the bar, poured myself another drink, and sat next to Mehtab, who looked at me with a playful smile.

"Why are we wasting time?" she said as she came over and sat in my lap.

She took the glass from me and set it on a side table. We began kissing, which gradually turned more aggressive and somewhat vicious. This time it felt less frenzied but more intimate and leisurely. Dinner remained untouched. Around one, I was asked to leave while Mehtab went into the bathroom for a shower. I dressed, took a plate, and served myself a lukewarm dinner. I sat quietly on the balcony and enjoyed my meal in peace while I heard Mehtab settle into her bed. Leaving the plate there, I walked back to my room. Just as I started to shower, it began to rain. It was like a lullaby as I fell into bed.

We left Tripura Castle the next morning at 8:30 am without having breakfast. Mr. Tarun and Teji Baruah were in the lounge to see us off. We needed to catch a late morning flight from Guwahati back to Delhi. At the airport, we had some sandwiches and coffee before boarding. The flight took off on time. During the flight, Mehtab discussed her travel plans.

"I've never felt so free," she said.

She also expressed her desire for her son Mansoor to take over from her. She mentioned that if that happens, she will want me around to guide and support him. I took this opportunity to remind her that I was merely an employee, and I had limited loyalty to the company. If I get a better opportunity, I might leave. If Mansoor doesn't like me, he could let me go.

"So, what do you suggest?" she asked.

"It's too early to think about it," I replied. "The situation you envision is at least six or seven years away," I continued. "Mansoor might decide to pursue something different. But we have plenty of time to decide," I concluded.

She fell silent for a time.

"You'll be there for me, won't you? In terms of business, I mean," she chuckled.

I kept my hand on hers and replied, "Always."

She closed her eyes and relaxed.

At the Delhi airport, Mehtab's car was waiting for her. I saw her off and took a taxi home. The events of the last three days ran through my mind. What a wonderful time I had! I then began to feel some guilt thinking of Priya. I had made a mistake, and it couldn't be undone. I justified it by thinking that as long as I stayed committed to looking after her, I was a loyal husband. It was a poor excuse, even to me.

Priya was happy to see me, and so were the kids. They were eager to hear all about the trip. I shared the wonderful experience and promised to take them to Shillong for a holiday. After dinner, we returned to our rooms. Priya seemed somewhat surprised by my enthusiasm that night.

"If this is what an official tour does to you, please go out more often," she giggled.

The next few days were primarily spent negotiating the deal with Omar, and it concluded amicably. Omar had little choice, as he wanted to escape the trap he was in. On one side were the authorities, while on the other lingered the threats and extortion from terrorist groups. He wanted to get away from it all, and he wanted to do so quickly. The funds were to be transferred to him both legitimately and through unregulated channels. Most of the cash would be delivered in tranches via 'Hawala'. Money would be given to an agency in India in rupees, and its equivalent would be provided to Omar abroad in foreign currency for a hefty commission, of course. Omar was planning to settle in Vancouver, where his wife had several relatives to support them. The change of ownership was slated for January 2002, after all payments had been made.

In November, we flew to Chandigarh to visit the Himachal plants. A middle-ranking manager was assigned by the Solan plant to receive us. We checked in at The Taj. Over the next two days, we were to drive to our plants near Solan and Kamarhati for inspections and return to Delhi on the fourth day. The Solan plant had hired a Mercedes taxi for our stay to transport us to and from the plant. The manager was staying at a different hotel. We enjoyed the anonymity of The Taj; no one knew us, which added to our sense of freedom. Mehtab and I picked up where we had left off in Shillong and had a great time. The plants were doing well but required maintenance. The visit followed the same schedule as in Shillong, minus the dinners with the GMs of the plants. We always returned to Chandigarh for the night. On the final day, Mehtab, apparently weary from the lengthy mountain drives, decided to retire early for the day.

"Ajay, I am tired," she said as she got out of the taxi. "I'd like to sleep early; you enjoy the bar," she suggested.

I didn't respond but escorted her to her floor and returned to my room to freshen up before heading to the bar. Her interest in me was waning, but I didn't mind at all. It showed that what we had was quite superficial, merely a need with no emotions involved. The next day, we returned to Delhi. I was so grateful to return to Priya and the kids.

Mehtab Under Threat

It was time to dispose of the massive amount of cash I had stashed away in my bank locker. I called Shiv Properties and made an appointment for the following Sunday. They would show us their upcoming apartments in the area. Priya and I arrived at Shiv Properties at eleven that Sunday. The staff treated us like potential high-end customers. We were shown various apartment buildings that were under construction and some nearing completion. Each location had a furnished model apartment to demonstrate what the finished apartment would look like. It was exhilarating to see these tastefully furnished dwellings. Priya admired a four-bedroom apartment with a servant room. It featured a large living and dining area with each bedroom having access to a bathroom. This particular property was nearing completion, and the common areas were already developed. The landscaping and gardens were fabulous. She looked at me questioningly and asked if the property would be beyond our budget. The agent interjected to say that HDFC Ltd, a housing loan financial organization, was in partnership with them. They would be happy to finance eighty percent of the purchase price after assessing our repayment capacity, of course. The agent explained the various payment plans while Priya explored the furnished apartment. He then drove us back to the office.

"I will return in a day or two to negotiate the price," I said, getting out of the car.

"Thank you, Sir," the agent replied.

On the drive back home, Priya remarked on how neat and tidy the apartments were. I pointed out that it had no children, no extra stuff, no extra crockery, pots, and pans that typically clutter a functional home. She agreed.

"Can we afford it?" she asked almost pleadingly after a long pause.

"Let me work it out," I replied. For the rest of the drive home, she stared out the window, perhaps daydreaming of her new home.

In the evening, I received a call from Mehtab. It was strange receiving a call from her on a Sunday. Something must be amiss, I thought.

"Ajay, I'm sorry to bother you on a Sunday, but it's important," she said.

"Go ahead," I prompted.

"Omar is having second thoughts about the deal. He called me to say he was reconsidering it," lamented Mehtab.

"I see," I replied. "Let me get to the bottom of this," I added.

"I thought I should let you know about the development as soon as possible," she said. "I'm hanging up now," she added.

"Good night," I answered, and she hung up.

I stayed near the phone for a while, wondering what had happened. I poured myself a drink and sat on the balcony to think. Just as I was settling down, the phone rang again. Priya answered the call this time. She called out to me, saying it was for me. I took the handset from her and said hello. It was Khanna on the other end.

"Hello Ajay, I have some urgent and bad news for you," he said.

My heart sank.

"Go ahead," I replied, trying not to reveal my dismay at his call.

"Mrs. Mattoo's life might be in danger."

He then explained that they had placed Omar's phone under surveillance for some time. Approximately four days ago, Omar informed his suppliers that he would soon be leaving the country, and that he was cancelling his orders with them. Conversations yesterday between him and one of the carpet suppliers revealed that militants were not happy with his decision. They wanted him to stay and continue supporting the jihad against India. They told him that if he encountered any problems, they would handle these. When Omar indicated he was facing some issues with Mehtab and that the intelligence agencies were aware of his activities, the militants assured Omar that soon Mehtab would no longer pose any problems and that the courts in India would have no proof linking anything back to Omar.

Khanna then asked me to ensure that Mehtab had some security and restrict her movements as much as possible. She should avoid any predictable schedule. He mentioned that he would keep me updated. I thanked him and returned to my drink. Mehtab's safety was of lesser concern to me. I could see my family's future going downhill if anything happened to her. Her safety was imperative, and ending the threat to her was key to my well-being.

While pondering the problem and sipping my whiskey, one question arose: Why would Omar let Mehtab know he was reconsidering the deal? She could have been eliminated without any warning. It struck me that we were set to sign a sale agreement with the transfer of some money to his bank in two days. He didn't want to enter into any agreement that would complicate things, whether Mehtab was alive or dead, so that was likely the reason. I had dinner in a sombre mood.

"Is everything alright?" Priya asked.

"Yes," I lied. "Just tired," I added.

That night, I couldn't sleep well at all. I pondered what immediate actions were necessary and how to eliminate the threat to Mehtab altogether, if possible. The next morning, I drove to Mehtab's house instead of the office. I explained the situation to her. She understood, as she was likely aware of her husband's shady past. We decided to hire personal armed security guards from a reputable security agency who would accompany her and be with her whenever she stepped out of the house. She agreed, though she detested the idea.

Back at the office, I informed Mr. Dubey and Mr. Rastogi that Mrs. Mattoo wouldn't be attending the office today. I then called a few security agencies and chose the one I thought was the best, hiring two gunmen for Mehtab's security. At least one would always be with her. How effective he would be in deterring an attack was another matter. They were to report for duty starting this afternoon. I called Khanna to inform him of the measures we had taken. I expressed that this security wasn't enough to ensure her safety and that more needed to be done. He seemed helpless. The government wouldn't provide police protection until we could demonstrate a tangible threat to her life.

"However, we can keep our ears and eyes open to ascertain when the threat escalates," he said.

I thanked him and began my routine office tasks absentmindedly, thinking about the sudden adverse situation and the possible solutions for it.

On Tuesday, Mehtab attended the office accompanied by her security guard. I thought Omar would have noticed this. What would he be thinking? He might wonder how the hell Mehtab knew that she was a marked woman. Why did she hire security? It would be interesting to know his reaction when he spoke to and questioned his masters in the valley (Kashmir). In the evening, while I was preparing to leave the office, I received another call from Khanna. He asked me to meet him in his office. I called Priya to inform her that I would be late. I then headed to Khanna's office. The office complex was empty, with locks on most offices. He was waiting for me and asked me to sit.

"I've been in touch with Mathur," Khanna said. "He informs me that telephone taps suggest that an amount of ten lakh rupees (approximately twenty-three thousand US dollars) has been settled for Mehtab's head. Omar will pay half of the agreed amount to the hit team in Delhi. The remaining amount will be settled by the carpet supplier on Omar's behalf once the team returns to Kashmir after completing the job.

Khanna then explained the plan he and Mathur had devised. Omar will likely assign one of his Kashmiri employees from his showroom to deliver the advance amount to the assassins at a location of their choosing. We intend to pick him up en route. You will subsequently impersonate him.

"Why me?" I asked.

"Because you speak Kashmiri, look Kashmiri, and won't disclose the plan to anyone," he replied.

He then went on to outline the rest of the plan. After confirming the rendezvous point with the employee, you will meet these individuals. Shortly thereafter, the Delhi Police Special Task Force (STF) personnel will arrive and apprehend the assassins. If they resist, then the inevitable will ensue.

"I might get caught in the crossfire if that happens," I pointed out.

"No, you won't," he assured me. "You will leave the money in the car. When the assassins question you about it, you will tell them that it's still in the car. Once you return to the car to retrieve it, the STF will enter the scene," he explained.

"It's far too risky," I protested.

"Well, all combat situations are," he replied dismissively.

It was my life on the line, not his, I thought. Yet, he was doing this for me and for his promising career. "Let's hope for the best," he said, getting up and extending his hand for a shake. I left the dismal government complex, mentally exhausted and shaken. I was being used as cannon fodder once again.

At home, I took a shower, poured myself a stiff whiskey, and tried to pretend to be cheerful with the kids and Priya. We discussed the new house that we would 'own' and the interiors that Priya and the children could plan. They were so excited that I had to remind them I had not yet finalized the deal or arranged the funds for the acquisition. This dampened their enthusiasm a bit. After dinner, I lay in bed with my back turned toward Priya, thinking about the events and how they would unfold. I heard Priya's gentle snoring; those snores were lullabies to me.

Bait Again

Wednesday passed normally. I was, of course, on edge since I didn't know when I would be called upon to be the bait again. Early Thursday morning, Khanna rang me up to say that the two assassins were on their way from Kashmir and expected to reach Delhi by Jhelum Express on Saturday. Jhelum Express seemed to be their favourite train. They would likely collect the money that same afternoon and execute their plan over the next few days after reconnaissance and planning. Our teams will be watching and waiting. My heart sank again, and my heartbeat increased. I was nervous. I wondered how long my luck would hold. I felt scared like never before. I immersed myself in work and kept busy for the next two days to keep thoughts of confronting the assassins at bay. On Friday evening, I requested a two-day leave from Mehtab over the phone. I mentioned that I was planning to acquire an apartment and needed to check out some sites.

"Okay," she said. "If there's some financial shortfalls, please don't hesitate to ask," she added before hanging up.

I hardly slept through the night. My mind kept racing with thoughts of what could go wrong. What questions might the assassins ask? What contingencies could arise, and how would I react to them? I think I finally drifted off around two in the morning. Priya woke me up because I had slept well past my usual time. She asked if I was well.

"Yes," I replied. "I don't have to go to the office today; I'm meeting some contractors later in the morning," I said, justifying my unusual behaviour.

While I was having breakfast, Khanna called. He suggested it would be a good idea for me to join their team in the operations room to stay updated.

The Jhelum Express entered Delhi at 9:30 a.m., just as I was leaving home. I arrived at Khanna's office by ten. He escorted me to a small hall cluttered with phones, satellite phones, and walkie-talkie devices. Several personnel were wearing headphones and monitoring phone traffic. Khanna and I settled into a corner table. Soon, a senior-looking man walked in, and Khanna stood up upon seeing him. I followed suit.

"So, is everything under control for today's operation?" he boomed.

"Yes, sir," Khanna replied. "The Task Force team is ready. They will conduct a quick recce (reconnaissance) of the area once we know where the money is being paid and devise their tactical plan," he added. "This is Mr. Ajay Raina, our decoy and my source," said Khanna, introducing me to the tall gentleman. "Our director," he said to me.

We shook hands.

"All the best then. I'll be waiting for the good news," he said before walking out.

At around half past ten, one of the operators informed Khanna that visual contact had been established with the targets. He provided their description and indicated where they were headed. They would most likely move towards the crowded Pahar Ganj area to check in at a budget hotel, as is their usual practice. Just a few minutes before noon, Khanna discovered where the assassins had checked in. Indeed, it was a cheap hotel in Pahar Ganj. At one o'clock, an operator signalled frantically to Khanna and started a tape recorder. Khanna picked up the headphones and began listening. After about six or seven minutes, Khanna removed the headphones. Ignoring me entirely, Khanna dialled a number.

After announcing himself, he stated, "Yes, we have the location and approximate time of the meeting point. The location is Bhudha Jayanti Car Park, and the time is five, just before it closes to the public," he said on the phone.

Bhudha Jayanti is a park located next to a reserve forest. It is an open area with lush green manicured gardens inside the boundary but forested outside and near the car park. The site was chosen well because it was merely ten to fifteen minutes from Mehtab's/Omar's residence. Listening to the conversation, my heart pounded heavily. The moment of reckoning was near. Khanna then turned to me with urgency,

"Do you have a short-sleeved blue sweater?" he asked.

"Yes," I answered.

"How long will it take to collect it from your home and be back?" he nearly shouted.

"About one and a half hours, could be two, depending on the traffic," I said.

"Shit," he swore.

He urged me to get up and walked out briskly with me in tow.

"Where's your car?" he yelled urgently. I pointed to my car in the parking lot about fifty yards away.

"Come on," he said, starting to run towards it.

I unlocked the car and got behind the wheel with equal urgency.

"Janpath," he shouted.

I sped out of the parking lot and headed for Janpath, which wasn't far. Khanna told me enroute that a 'Bashir Ahmed,' wearing a blue short-sleeved sweater, was to deliver the money. We arrived at Janpath in about twenty minutes. It took us another half hour to buy the blue short-sleeved sweater.

We returned around two-thirty. "Anything new?" asked Khanna, entering the operating room.

"Everything is tied up, sir," an operator replied. "It is confirmed that Omar's salesperson is Bashir Ahmed. He will take the cash to the assassins. He is travelling in a blue Maruti Suzuki 800."

"What's the latest news of the assassins?" asked Khanna.

"Sir, a person was seen handing over a battered, white Ambassador car number HNC 2047 to one of the assassins outside their hotel," replied the operator

As this information was being relayed to Khanna by the operators, I felt as though I was being dragged to the gallows. I felt miserable and thought I might faint.

"Put on your sweater," Khanna instructed.

He walked out with me again. This time, we were driving in his government Gypsy. We were heading to the Diplomatic Enclave where Mehtab's and Omar's residences are located. We stopped about half a kilometre from their house. There were traffic police on both sides of the road, pretending to check vehicles. At around four-fifteen, a blue Maruti Suzuki car emerged from the Mattoo house, driven by a lone individual wearing a blue short-sleeved sweater. He proceeded towards Sardar Patel Road. As he neared the policemen, he slowed down. They waved him down and directed him to the side. The driver, Bashir Ahmed, was instructed to step out of the car. The keys were taken from him, and I was told to get in and drive to the Buddha Jayanti Car Park. The Gypsy followed with the actual Bashir Ahmed inside it.

I headed to the destination with my heart racing and feeling nervous. I arrived in the parking lot a little before five and began searching for a parking spot. Most vehicles were leaving the parking lot as darkness approached. I noticed a white Ambassador HNC 2047 parked on a track just outside the car park. I drove towards it but parked my car well away within the car park limits. I got out and looked around. Two guys waved to me from about fifty or sixty yards away and gestured for me to approach them. They were near the edge of the forested area away from the visitors leaving the park. When I noticed their cocky attitude, I felt disgusted and angry. These people were prepared to kill innocents for their petty ends. If I had been armed, I would have taken them down myself. It would amount to murder, though.

My fear began to recede. It was time for action, but I was still a little nervous. I approached them, and when I was close, one of them asked me who I was in Kashmiri. "Bashir," I replied.

"Bashir Ahmed," I repeated. "Omar *sahib* sent me," I said.

"*Salamawalekum*," said the taller guy.

"*Waalaikumasslam*", I answered.

"Where's the money?" he asked in Kashmiri.

"In the car," I answered.

Their shirts were not tucked in. One could see the bulges where they carried the pistols.

"Your Kashmiri sounds different," said the other fellow.

My legs nearly gave way.

"I've been in Delhi for decades; my accent has perhaps got corrupted," I answered in as good a Kashmiri accent as I could muster. "I will get the money," I said, turning away.

"No! Stop!" said the taller of the two. "He'll get it," he said, pointing to his shorter companion. "You stay here and give him the key," the tall one ordered.

I handed the key to the shorter guy, wondering what came next.

"What number?" asked the guy collecting the keys.

My heart skipped a beat. I didn't know the number of the car I drove in here.

"It's the blue Maruti over there," I said.

"You don't know the number?" asked the big fellow.

"It's not my car; I was instructed to drive it here to give you the money. The car belongs to the house supervisor," I said. The guy with the car keys started to head for the blue car.

As he neared the car, two police vehicles, followed by Khanna's Gypsy, emerged and came to a screeching halt. About ten armed policemen from the Task Force, dressed in civilian clothes but wearing bulletproof vests, jumped out and tried to grab the shorter guy heading for my car. He turned back and ran toward where we were standing. The taller guy pulled out a pistol, cocked it, and fired several rounds towards the Task Force before fleeing towards the forest area. I knelt with my hands in the air. Bullets were now being fired from both sides. The assassins ran towards some bushes, away from the car park. Here, another group of Task Force guys were waiting, and they opened fire on the assassins. It was a perfect ambush. The two tried to run in another direction when the shorter one was struck by bullets, and the taller one collapsed a few feet away. He had tried to raise his hands, but it was too late. Bullets were being pumped in from two directions. Suddenly, the fire stopped. Khanna hauled me up and took me away. I saw a police officer retrieve the shorter guy's pistol, which he hadn't been able to draw. The officer cocked it and fired two shots into the ground before throwing it next to him. The cameraman accompanying the Task Force began taking photos. I was in shock, and so was the real Bashir Ahmed, who was trembling in Khanna's Gypsy. The few people still in the car park ran helter-skelter.

Khanna looked at Bashir.

"You've done well, Bashir," he said in Hindi. "You gave us a good tip," he added.

Bashir had pissed in his pants upon witnessing the encounter.

"I did nothing, *sahib*," he said, sobbing.

"Listen closely," Khanna began slowly. "You and Omar *sahib* gave us the tip, and we bumped these guys off. "That is the story that will reach Kashmir," he said, shaking Bashir by the arm. "Convey this to Omar *sahib*."

Bashir did not answer. Khanna handed me some water from a bottle he carried in his vehicle. I took a gulp or two and passed it to Bashir, who declined it, still sobbing. Khanna instructed Bashir to get down. Supporting him with his elbow, Khanna helped him to his car. The car keys lay on the ground a few feet away. Khanna picked them up and opened the car door. He retrieved the briefcase containing the money and told Bashir to sit and drive away. Bashir started the car and drove out of the parking lot very slowly. An ambulance arrived, possibly prepositioned some distance away in case injuries occurred to either side. After placing the briefcase in his vehicle, Khanna approached the leader of the STF. They conversed for a few minutes before shaking hands. Khanna returned to his Gypsy, and we drove out of the parking lot. I could see the two bodies being taken towards the ambulance.

As Khanna drove back to his office car park, he didn't speak much but seemed pleased with himself after the successful operation.

"You handled the situation very well," he said, breaking his silence. I did not answer. "The blokes made a big mistake by selecting this isolated spot," he added.

"Why could you not use Bashir or one of your own operatives? Why did you make me risk my life by replacing him?" I asked rather rudely.

Khanna was silent for a while.

"Bashir could have signalled to the assassins that there was trouble; he could have panicked or even run away. With him, there were far too many uncertainties," he explained. "We don't have any Kashmiri or Kashmiri-speaking operatives in the Delhi area who could have been mustered for the operation on such short notice," he added. "You, on the other hand, are seasoned bait," he laughed.

I was not amused at all. In the parking lot, he paused near my car for me to get out, then drove away with the five lakh rupees (over eleven thousand US dollars) taken from the encounter site. Would he keep all of it for himself, share it with the Task Force, or surrender it to the Government? I wondered.

As I got into my car, I realized that the wait for the encounter had been long and exhausting, but the encounter itself was short and clean. Once again, I was happy to be alive. I reached home just before eight, had a shower, and changed into my *pyjamas*. Feeling hungry, I poured myself a drink and made my way to the dining table. Priya told me to help myself from the kitchen.

"I think we need a full-time servant now," I said in protest.

After dinner, I watched the news to see if the encounter had been covered by the media yet. It hadn't. Perhaps the late-night news would carry it. Lacking the patience to wait that long, I went to bed. I slept well.

I woke up a little late. Priya was already sitting on the balcony reading the newspaper with a teapot and two cups by her side. I joined her.

"You know, two terrorists were shot in an encounter last night, here in Delhi," she said, alarmed, just as I began pouring my tea.

I took the Sunday paper from her and saw that the encounter was one of the major headlines.

"Two terrorists gunned down near Bhudha Jayanti Park," it read. It went on to describe that based on specific intelligence inputs, the Delhi Police STF cornered the terrorists. A gunfight ensued, and the two terrorists were killed. Two Task Force personnel also sustained injuries in the firefight. The identities of those killed are being ascertained. It is suspected that they were affiliated with a Pakistani *tanseem* (terrorist organization) operating in Kashmir.

'Injuries?' I thought. Well, one could always get bandaged to fake these to add credibility to the encounter. It was a real encounter, though. Bullets were fired first by the assassins.

Omar Panics

While we were having breakfast, I got a phone call from Mehtab.

"What did you do?" she asked after the initial hello.

"What did I do?" I questioned in return.

"Omar met me rather early in the morning," she said. "He seemed distressed and anxious. It looks like he hasn't slept in days. He wants our deal finalized today so he can leave for Canada tonight. He seems quite panicked," she said, sounding alarmed.

I held back an urge to laugh. It was very mean of me to be amused at his plight.

"It is a Sunday," I reminded Mehtab.

"That's the point. He was reconsidering the deal. Now, he wants it done posthaste," she said. "You must have done something," she added accusingly.

"I'll come over at ten and meet him," I replied.

I arrived at Mehtab's house at ten. Instead of entering her home, I took the external stairs to Omar's floor. I rang the bell, and a servant appeared. I mentioned I was there to see Omar *sahib*. He asked me to take a seat on the *veranda* and went inside to inform him. Omar came out almost immediately. Mehtab was right. He looked utterly distressed, with red eyes, stooping shoulders, and an air of vulnerability. I stood up as a gesture of respect.

Initially, he glared at me, which was understandable. Then he invited me to sit. We did not shake hands.

"You're in cahoots with the intelligence agencies, aren't you?" he accused. "Bashir told me everything," he continued.

I did not answer.

"You made it appear as if I tipped off the police," he added accusingly. "These guys will kill me if I stick around here any longer. I want the agreement signed today," he said, getting straight to the point.

"Omar *sahib*, it's a Sunday; the courts and registration offices are closed," I began calmly. "No one will act against you so soon. It will take days, if not weeks, for the *tanseem* to know what exactly happened. It will take even more time for them to plan any revenge attack. They know they have been compromised and cannot afford to risk sending in another team to be eliminated by the police so soon. They must be in shock themselves," I tried to reassure him.

He seemed to register my reasoning.

"We will request our lawyers today to have the paperwork ready for tomorrow. In the meantime, we will arrange the funds," I suggested. "You could fly out on Monday night or on Tuesday after signing the agreement.

He seemed to have relaxed a little, but then he confronted me accusingly, "You have uprooted me."

This blew my fuse.

"You! You conspired to have Mehtab killed," I almost yelled at him, pointing my finger at his face.

I could feel my face twist with anger.

"I could have you arrested today for attempted murder and for conspiring with terrorists," I continued, fully aware that proving such charges in a court of law would be very difficult.

He was shaken by now.

"I'm sorry," he squeaked, alarm writ large on his face.

I regained my composure and concluded, "Thank your stars that Mehtab is being so considerate and kind."

"Alright, we'll sign the agreement on Monday," he said before standing up.

He extended his hand this time. We shook hands, and I descended the stairs while he waited on the *veranda* to see me leave.

I now rang the doorbell at Mehtab's house. The servant ushered me in, and Mehtab appeared almost immediately, fresh from her Sunday bath.

"The agreement will be signed on Monday," I informed her matter-of-factly.

"So abrupt!" she pointed out.

"I'm sorry, I had a rough morning with Omar," I said apologetically.

"Some tea?" she offered. I declined.

"I will speak with your lawyer and let him know," I said, indicating that I would like to leave.

"Alright, have a great Sunday," she said as I walked away.

Back home, I called her lawyer, who said he would be ready with the agreement documents. I spent the rest of the day relaxing. The news of the encounter. The distortions of facts the news portals presented were incredible.

Monday saw a flurry of activity at the Mattoo residence. A bank draft, as earnest money, was handed over to Omar. Additionally, part of the promised cash was given to him in two large suitcases. He signed the agreement to sell his portion of the property to Mehtab. The final registration of the transfer would be completed by January 2002 after full payment. The agreement outlined the total amount agreed upon to ensure that no one would back out. However, the final registration would reflect the amount that both parties choose to declare to the tax authorities. The agreement will subsequently be destroyed. A significant sum of money paid will remain off the record. I assumed Omar would hand over the cash received to his agent in India, and he would receive an equivalent amount in Canadian currency.

The most important document signed that afternoon was an affidavit by Omar relinquishing his claim to all businesses of the late Farookh Ahmed Mattoo or his heirs. Not only did Mehtab save her business, but she also acquired the entire Mattoo residence for herself and her children. Everyone left by around four. Mehtab requested that tea be served to the two of us on the veranda. As we sat down, she placed her hand on mine.

"A big thank you to you, Ajay," she said sincerely. "You have achieved the impossible in such a short time and with ease," she continued.

"Anything for you, Mehtab," I replied.

She was unaware that I had risked my life for her. The tea was served with some exquisite cookies.

While we were having tea, she offered me the cookies. I took one.

"You risked your life in the encounter for me," she said appreciatively.

I was surprised to hear this. I was under the impression that she wouldn't know about my involvement in the encounter and how I had risked my life, but she did. I was so wrong.

"I knew what you were up to," she continued. "I could see it all in Omar's behaviour," she added.

"Please don't ever mention it again for the sake of your safety and mine," I replied.

We had our tea in silence thereafter.

"These last two days have been very hectic," I said as I got up to leave.

She also stood up and hugged me. It was a hug of gratitude. Back home, I felt cheerful. Priya was curious, and I told her that Omar had withdrawn his claim to Farookh's business and Mehtab had signed a deal to acquire his share of the Mattoo House, making her the sole owner.

"I must ring her up and congratulate her," she said excitedly.

I asked her not to.

"She's tired today; call her tomorrow," I advised.

I then brought up the subject of the new apartment we were planning to acquire. Priya grew excited and broke out into a chatter of what she was contemplating in the new apartment she liked. I listened to her intently. It was my way of distracting myself from the recent events.

I met the owner of Shiv Property the next day without informing Priya. I negotiated a favourable deal. The owner of Shiv Property and I went to the HDFC Ltd office and finalized the loan amount and repayment terms. I handed over the full cash that was stashed in the bank locker and received a receipt for it. The standard agreement was signed, and one copy was given to me in a large festive envelope. The possession was expected a month before Diwali, about ten months away. After the deal, I went to the office to catch up on pending work.

Upon arriving home, I handed the agreement envelope to Priya.

"Here, your very own new home," I said, smiling.

She looked utterly surprised. Her expression gradually shifted from shock to happiness. It took her a moment to fully grasp the enormous news. The children, having overheard our conversation, rushed out of their rooms, all excited. I had to repeat what I had told their mother. Priya took out the agreement as if to read it but then pushed it back into the envelope without reading a single word. Joy filled the house, accompanied by much happy commotion. There were numerous questions, but only a few answers from me that evening.

The next morning, Mehtab arrived late to the office. She called me into her chamber.

"Omar left last night with his wife and a considerable amount of luggage. He mentioned that he was leaving the floor in my care until the final possession is officially handed over to me. He also requested that I absorb his staff into my team, and I agreed. I went up to see the floor this morning, met the staff, and provided them with some instructions. It was kind of him to trust me like that," she said sadly. "Many things will need to be sorted out," she noted. "Thank you once again."

"Take your time sorting it out, Mehtab. There is no rush now." I replied before returning to my chamber.

The immediate threat to Mehtab had been taken care of but the long-term threat remained. For this threat to cease, Mehtab needed to sever Farookh's and Omar's connection to the terrorist groups. This connection was Omar's carpet manufacturer and supplier, Ashrav Mir, owner of Oriental Carpets based in Srinagar.

I would have to ask Khanna for another favour, I thought. Such favours from him were fraught with danger for me. Nevertheless, I spoke to him to express my gratitude for the pre-emptive action he had planned and executed so brilliantly. I used this opportunity to stroke his ego and asked him if there was a way to ensure Mehtab's safety for good. I suggested that if the link between the Mattoo family and the go-between were broken, this would insulate her from the threat.

He was silent for a moment and then replied, "Can be arranged."

I did not want to discuss the matter further, fearing that he might use me as bait again.

The beginning of December saw both Rajiv Dubey and Arun Rastogi tender their resignations. They wanted to leave this 'bloody' company. The events of the past few months, starting with my abduction, had frightened them. They had found greener pastures with other multinational firms. In turn, we hired two young men in their early thirties with MBAs from IIMs (Indian Institutes of Management). This shift in the hierarchy made me the most senior employee at the head office. I was now running the show and began to consolidate my position.

December 15th was a Friday. That evening, I was catching up on the national news while enjoying my usual drink. Breaking news flashed across the screen: some unknown gunmen had shot and killed Ashrav Meer, the owner of Oriental Carpets, as he was returning from Friday prayers. The report stated that no one had claimed responsibility for the attack yet, but the involvement of militants was suspected. He had been receiving extortion threats lately. I absorbed the news with utter surprise. Then my phone rang. It was Khanna.

"Your work is done," he said without even exchanging pleasantries.

"Thank you, Khanna *sahib*," I replied.

"Enjoy your evening," he remarked before hanging up.

I was in a state of shock, elated, and happy all at once. I wished Mehtab knew what I had accomplished for her. The threat to her life was hopefully over.

The next day, all the papers also carried the news of Ashrav Meer. He was described as a philanthropist and a prominent local figure. The papers also mentioned the extortion threat he had received a few days earlier, which he did not report to the police. They went on to say that no one had taken responsibility for his assassination so far.

Elevation

Late in the morning, while I was at the office, Mehtab rang me up.

"Hi Ajay, I can't thank you enough. You amaze me," she said. "I don't want you to deny anything. I know it all," she continued.

"Anything else?" I asked her, unsure of what to say.

"I am planning a two-month trip abroad. You will have to take care of everything completely," she told me. I am also promoting you to the position of Executive Managing Director of the company. "

My heart raced, and my head felt light.

"That would make me equal, if not senior, to the guys heading the plants, and they won't like it," I pretended to object.

"I have spoken to them, and they have agreed," she replied. "They might think of it as Kashmiri nepotism," she laughed.

She ended the call by congratulating me and asking me to work out my own compensation package and submit it for her approval.

"Be reasonable," she laughed again, wrapping up the conversation.

I kept this information from Priya because I didn't want any premature celebrations. Happy things were happening, and they were happening fast. I was superstitious, as most Indians are.

On Monday, an office memo drafted by the new HR Head and signed by Mehtab announced my elevation to everyone in the company, including the GMs of the plants. I was now practically number two in the company. I broke the news to Priya, saying that Mehtab had given me added responsibility and that it was not fair on her part to put the entire load on my shoulders. Priya sympathized with me and tried to change the topic to help me cope. I knew she would be mad at me when other ladies began to congratulate her.

2001 began with the company performing well. The demand for juice was increasing by leaps and bounds, with the aerated drinks being relegated to the lower category of beverages. The financial year concluded on 31 March with positive financial results. The company was in the final stages of acquiring land for the fourth plant in Nasik, where grape juice would be processed and packaged. Some additional land would be set aside for the winery that we planned to add to our products in the coming years.

In September, we took possession of our new four-bedroom apartment. Priya went berserk trying to do it up. We moved into our new abode on October 6 after the customary 'Grah Pravesh puja', a thanksgiving prayer before one begins living in a new dwelling. It was a festive occasion. Mehtab attended the function and asked Priya how much we had spent on the furniture. Priya provided an approximate figure.

As Mehtab was leaving the function, she handed Priya an envelope.

"*Shagun*," said Mehtab briefly.

Shagun is money given to the homeowner as a blessing for the house.

When we checked the envelope that evening, we found a cheque for a little over what Priya had spent on buying all the furniture for the house. It was substantial. Priya teared up with emotion and called Mehtab to thank her for being so generous.

"I have given you far less than what I have taken from you, Priya," Mehtab said, almost confessing in a way.

We, as a family, were thrilled at the prospect of celebrating this year's Diwali in November in our very own house.

Mehtab had started to travel extensively. Her freedom from Farookh, an abundance of funds, and her curiosity prompted her to explore new places. With her charm and beauty, she was a celebrity wherever she went, and she relished this status. Just before Christmas, I was approached by a rival firm, a much larger publicly listed company offering a very attractive compensation package, which I declined. Although their offer surpassed the generous package I was receiving as the Executive MD, I couldn't enjoy the same freedom I had with Nectar Juices. Mehtab learned about this offer and invited me to her home for a private conversation.

She asked what it would take to keep me permanently with the company.

"Just an assurance that I won't be kicked out when Mansoor takes over from you," I replied.

An uncomfortable silence followed.

"How can we address this?" she inquired after a moment.

"I could be part of the company," I suggested.

"That's an excellent idea," Mehtab responded, almost beaming with enthusiasm. I smiled in response.

"What share would be sufficient to keep you as a partner?" she asked, feigning seriousness.

"How much do you think I'm worth?" I responded, grinning.

She looked at me playfully. "To me personally, not much, but to the company, a lot," she said with a slight smile.

"Make it worth my while," I replied. "Would ten percent be enough?" she proposed.

Ten percent was substantial. Given the company's current assets and future potential, it was worth millions of dollars. However, it felt a little below my perceived worth.

"Okay," I said somewhat nonchalantly.

Mehtab placed her lovely hand on mine and said, "Quote your price, '*meri jaan*' (my life)."

"I will not," I replied.

"Will fifteen percent be enough as an incentive?" she asked.

I was taken aback by the offer. Straight fifty percent jump! I felt as if I were robbing her and Mansoor.

"That's a very generous offer," I stated.

"Welcome aboard, partner," she said, smiling.

"I am committing daylight robbery," I confessed.

"I am purchasing my freedom, a carefree life, your loyalty, and the company's future, all in one go," she replied. "It's settled then. Ask the Company Secretary to work out the details and prepare a proposal. Draw up the paperwork before the financial year ends in March," she said decisively.

"So, when do we go for another visit?" she asked, shifting the topic and showering me with her charm. "Let's go to Nasik," she suggested before I could respond.

We enjoyed lunch together in her spacious dining hall. I left her home around 3 PM, feeling millions of dollars richer.

The trip to Nasik was fruitful in many ways. We had a wonderful time and successfully identified a large piece of land about thirty miles from Nasik at a very reasonable price. After finalizing the finances, I was set to execute the deal in six weeks. My life had taken an incredible turn for the better, and I had reached heights I had never imagined possible.

Being '*deadly*' had truly paid off.

Epilogue

June 2014

The new government was in place. It was considered a government with integrity. New measures were to be adopted to curb corruption. Bypassing taxation to create illegitimate funds was to be considered taboo. Nectar Juices recognized the need for a change in its financial dealings. We decided to do away with generating unaccounted cash. The result was that we were able to show astounding profits in our books. The company was an excellent investment option. It was a good time to go public. The public issue was likely to be an inevitable success. The public funds were intended to expand our winery in Nasik, start a new coconut juice plant near Kochi, and establish a tomato puree plant near Amritsar, Punjab. Four years ago, we had moved into a larger complex in a newer building, and now the company would require another floor to accommodate a board of directors. I was set to become the CEO of the company, and I personally planned to acquire about three or four percent more shares to secure my future within the company.

Mansoor had started his own international software company and was doing very well. He did not seem interested in the juice business. Farhana Mattoo, a young lady of astounding beauty, was married to an American Kashmiri tycoon. She wasn't interested in India because she found it too corrupt, chaotic, and dirty.

Omar and his family were well established in Canada. He now had a chain of carpet showrooms, ironically called Oriental Carpets. These were spread all over the Americas and Europe. He imports carpets and rugs from countries like India, Iran, and Turkey.

Mr. Resham Khanna was heading the Intelligence Bureau. We enjoyed getting together at the Delhi Gymkhana occasionally.

Shyama Khan was still employed by the company in the same position on a significantly improved package.

Kashmir remained as volatile as ever. Political shifts in India's approach towards Kashmir militancy were expected from the new regime in India.

My children, Rohan and Rhea, were pursuing their higher education in the US and were unlikely to return to India except during holidays.

Mehtab, who seemed ageless, had charmed politicians to become a Member of Parliament (MP) in the Rajya Sabha (the Upper House). It was a highly prestigious position with little work or accountability. All she was expected to do was be present in the Rajya Sabha when crucial bills were to be passed and vote for whatever her party was adopting as the law.

I look back in shame at the time I wept like a coward in the face of death, but I also look back with pride at my redemption. I acted and reacted, and I avenged myself.

I remembered the powerful proverb from the Rajputana province of India:

'Veer Bhogya Vasundhara,'

'The Courageous Inherit the Earth.'

About the Author

This novel is a debutant effort by Avinder Singh. The author has served in Kashmir during his career. He has used his experience and knowledge of the area, the circumstances and the general situation prevailing at the time in Kashmir and India in the year 2000 to create this work of fiction.

www.ingramcontent.com/pod-product-compliance
Lightning Source LLC
Chambersburg PA
CBHW030242200626
46816CB00002BA/475